what
boys
really
want

PETE HAUTMAN

what
boys
really
want

?

SCHOLASTIC PRESS ● NEW YORK

Library of Congress Cataloging-in-Publication Data available

ISBN 978-0-545-11315-1

10 9 8 7 6 5 4 3 2 1   12 13 14 15 16

Printed in the U.S.A.   23
First edition, January 2012

The text was set in Chaparral Pro with Adrianna Extended Pro Light.
Book design by Christopher Stengel

In memory of Rene,
a boy who always knew
exactly what he wanted.

Chapter One
THE SKANK FACTOR

Miz Fitz,

My boyfriend is always saying stupid stuff. How can I fix him?
— Angie

Miz Fitz sez:

Get a dog. Fixing a dog is easier.

ADAM

The idea for the book came to me as a bunch of us were tubing down the Apple River on a nice, sunny day, the last weekend before school started. Lita had hooked her legs over my inner tube and was yakking about how Emily Vernon was totally obsessed with Dennis Long, and what did I think about that, and do you think she should ask him out, and blah blah blah.

"Emily is pissing into the wind," I told Lita.

That shut her up for a second.

"I guess you have to be a guy to get that," I said.

Her eyes rolled and at the same time her eyebrows squeezed together. Lita Wold has a very mobile face with big, hazel eyes and slightly sharp features, kind of like a stern, curly-brown-haired elf. She is the exact opposite of a tall, straight-blond-haired male. That's what I am.

"Don't worry, I *get* it." She kicked away from my tube, sending us bobbing in opposite directions.

I figured Lita wouldn't be able resist continuing our conversation, and I was right. A minute later she paddled back.

"Dennis doesn't like Emily at *all*?" she said.

"He's hot for that new girl. Blair."

We hit an eddy and spun around; now I was facing upstream.

"Not Blair Thompson!" she said.

"Yeah."

"Isn't she kind of skanky?"

"I'll find out," I said. I kicked off from Lita's inner tube.

"Hey!" Lita shouted, spinning off toward the bank as I paddled back to Bob Glaus and Robbie Conseco, who were sharing an enormous tractor-tire inner tube and a six-pack of beer. Robbie had offered me one, but I don't like warm beer. Actually, I don't like it much cold, either.

"Hey, Robbie," I said. "How do you rate that Blair Thompson?"

"On what scale?"

"Skank Factor, scale of one to ten."

"Which way does the scale read?"

"One would be the Virgin Mary. Ten is walking roadkill."

"I give her a six," said Robbie. "Slightly skanky."

Bob said, "No way! She's at least a nine."

I didn't really know Blair, but I thought nine was a bit high.

2

"Thanks." I paddled after Lita.

"Seven point five," I said when I caught up with her.

"Seven point five what?"

I explained the Skank Scale.

"So how do you get seven point five?" she asked.

"You take the average of Robbie's and Bob's ratings. Seven point five."

"What about you?"

"Me?"

"How do you rate her?"

Something in her voice told me I had to be careful. "I don't really know her," I said.

"What about me? You *do* know me. How do I score on your skank-o-meter?"

Uh-oh, I thought, looking at her now-flattened eyes and tight mouth. When Lita got all horizontal in the face, it was best to tread cautiously.

"I don't think the scale applies to you," I said.

"I'm not even a little bit skanky?" Her eyes got impossibly narrower.

Double uh-oh. Suddenly, I wasn't even sure what skanky *meant.* Also, with Lita, it was a fine line between scratch-your-eyes-out mad and just-kidding-around mad, and I wasn't sure where she was at.

"Uh . . . you want me to poll Robbie and Bob?"

"No, jerkball, I do *not* want you to poll Robbie and Bob. I just want to know how skanky you think I am."

"How skanky do you want to be? I mean, what would make you happy? A two? Three?"

Lita glared at me but with a little twinkle that told me it was a fake glare, so I kept talking.

3

"Eleven point three? Negative six?"

Her face loosened and she laughed. I was on a roll.

"Two to the power of zilch?"

"All of the above," she said. "Tell me something, Adam — what do you really want?"

"Me?" I asked, trying to buy some time.

"You as in *boys*. Adolescent males. All of you."

At least we weren't still on the Skank Scale.

"Fast cars, fast women, and a kick-ass sound system," I said.

"I don't believe that," Lita said, giving me her thou-shalt-not-bullshit-me look.

"Well, it's true," I said. "I'd definitely rather be riding around in a Ferrari with a hot babe right now than floating down this stupid river."

"Thanks a lot." Lita unhooked her legs from my tube and kicked herself away. "First you tell me I'm skanky, then you tell me I'm stupid."

"I never said either of those things!"

"I know what you said."

Lita is practically the smartest person I know, but she can be highly irrational at times. I never said she was skanky, I just asked her how skanky she wanted to be. And I never called her stupid. I said the river was stupid. But arguing with Lita is like trying to eat an ice-cream cone from the bottom up. Very messy.

Chapter Two
SELECTIVE MEMORIES

Girls complain that guys are thoughtless, rude, and self-centered. That is sometimes true. But girls should remember that sometimes guys are thoughtful, polite, and generous. That's the secret to true happiness in a relationship — remember the good things.

— **from** *What Boys Want*

LITA

I met Adam Merchant in kindergarten when he pulled a bullfrog out of his Ninja Turtles backpack and shoved it in my face. I don't think he was trying to scare me. It was just his idea of being friendly. But I didn't take it that way. I don't know what I was thinking. Maybe I'd been watching some violent cartoons or something. Instead of screaming or bursting into tears like any normal frog-frightened five-year-old, I hit him in the face with my Pokémon lunch box. There was blood everywhere and lots of crying. You can still see the scar when his forehead gets tan.

We were just little kids, though, so it seemed perfectly natural that the next day Adam and I became best friends, and we've been tight ever since.

That's not to say that Adam is perfect. Far from it. For one thing, he has a selective memory. I suppose that's what makes him so unbearably *cheerful* all the time. I'd be cheery, too, if I only remembered things precisely the way I wanted. And wouldn't it be delightful if every time you stumbled across somebody else's good idea you thought it was *you* who'd had it?

For example, that day on the Apple River? The day when a whole crew of us decided tornado-watch-be-damned we were going tubing down the Apple one last time before the end of summer? Adam insists it was sunny and warm and wonderful and we all had a lovely time. Ha!

Here are the True Facts. First, Robbie and Bob started guzzling beer before we had even rented our tubes, and there was this awkward scene in the parking lot where I had to practically wrestle Bob to get him to give me his car keys because I knew if I waited until he got loaded I'd never get hold of them. Then five minutes after we got in the water, the temperature dropped ten degrees and it started to drizzle.

The Apple River isn't that big. In most places you can easily wade across it. Even the rapids are just mini-rapids. The rocks are smooth, there are no deadly whirlpools, and hardly anybody drowns. The bad thing is that once you start down the river there's No Turning Back. The banks are a tangle of poison ivy and nettles and prickly bushes, so even if the weather suddenly turns to thunder and hail, you have to keep floating all the way to the end, an hour-long journey and no way to speed it up.

Believe me, it was *cold*.

But Adam blocks all that out.

Example number two: Adam *still* thinks he got his idea for the book while floating down the Apple. The fact is, the book idea started two weeks earlier when we were watching *The Lord of the Rings* on his parents' inadequate little TV. During one of the tedious parts (there are several), Adam said that when he got rich he would buy a plasma-screen TV for every room in his house.

"I could get rich if I wrote a book like *The Lord of the Rings*. How hard can it be? You just make stuff up."

"It's not that easy," I said, speaking from experience. I had myself been working on a novel for some time, an edgy romance set in an alternate universe. The title kept changing but usually it contained the words *Wrath* and/or *Lust*. If my dad were pitching it to a movie studio (not that I would ever show it to him), he might describe it as *Pride and Prejudice* meets *Gossip Girl* meets *Harry Potter*. Except he'd probably leave out the *Pride and Prejudice* part. I had some great characters, but I'd been having trouble with the story. In fact, I hadn't worked on the novel in months. Not since I'd started blogging, which was somewhat addictive.

Adam was fast-forwarding through one of the boring parts.

"I just can't see you sitting and typing for hundreds of hours," I said. "You're far too distractible."

"I could do it," Adam said, brimming with Adam confidence. "Elves with flying broomsticks and intelligent dinosaurs. I'd put some zombies in there, too."

"If you want to get rich," I told him, "you should write an advice book. Tell people how to lose weight or be happy or whatever. Notice how hardly anybody's fat in this movie? *The Middle Earth Diet — Why Elves Don't Get Fat.* Guaranteed instant bestseller."

Adam hit the PAUSE button on the remote. "Really?"

"Sure. Or better yet, write a book explaining why boys are such idiots."

He laughed, and *that* was when the idea of becoming a bestselling advice author began to crystallize in Adam's forever-strategizing mind. Of course he never stopped to think that *I* was the one who was destined to become a Famous Author or that *I* had given him the idea for the book in the first place.

But if he wanted to think it all started on a warm sunny day on the Apple River, I was not about to shatter his delusion. Arguing with Adam Merchant is as useless as climbing up a down escalator. Maybe you get to the top eventually, but it's exhausting, and the escalator just keeps on going.

ADAM

We were floating down the river on our tubes, Lita a couple yards away from me, half a mile yet to go.

"What do *you* think boys want?" I asked. One sure way to cheer up Lita is to ask for her opinion. There's nothing she likes better.

She thought for a moment. Lita can get a lot of thinking done in very few seconds.

"Well," she said at last, "boys like to think they're wonderful and funny."

"I already *know* I'm wonderful and funny."

Lita gave me her one-raised-eyebrow look.

"You laugh at my jokes," I pointed out.

"Ha! Girls are *taught* to laugh at boys' stupid jokes. Right after potty training."

"Yeah, right. Hey, y'know what would make a great advice book? A book about what guys and girls really think. Instead of just guessing all the time, you could look it up."

"Who's going to write it? You? I don't think —"

She was interrupted by a howl from Robbie. Their tube, now about twenty yards ahead of us, tilted and bucked.

"Rapids!" Lita yelled.

My inner tube dipped and rose and tilted; the current caught my feet and spun me as Lita shrieked in an Oh-Crap-I'm-Gonna-Die sort of way, and our tubes collided and sprang apart. We were both laughing, and we collided again, but this time my tube slid up over hers and then seemed to pop right out from under me, leaving me flailing in the swift-moving water.

"Lita!" I yelled, and got a mouthful of river water.

A few seconds later my feet found the sandy bottom, and I was thigh deep in the water, leaning into the current just below the rapids, my tube jouncing away downstream. Lita, a few yards away, still hanging on to her tube, was laughing so hard that for two whole seconds I thought she was crying.

LITA

I have been learning to keep my true thoughts to myself. Mostly I succeed, with the exception of the occasional blurt. That day on the Apple River I really tried to not jump all over Adam when he brought up the book thing, even though I was thinking a) it was a stupid idea, b) Adam was not smart enough to write a book, and c) it was My Idea in the first place.

I don't mean Adam isn't intelligent. He is not nearly as unaware as most boys, which puts him a good three notches above your average chimpanzee. But he is not what you would call *book smart*. Reading and writing is *my* department. Adam is strictly ADD. One time he asked me to help him write a book report on *The Catcher in the Rye*.

"Did you read the book?" I asked.

"Most of it."

"How much is 'most' of it?"

"Almost the whole first chapter," he said.

"You didn't even finish one chapter?"

"I thought that Holden Caulfield guy was kind of whiny."

You can see why the idea of him writing an entire book struck me as ludicrous. Not that he doesn't have his good points. Adam is one of the few guys who ever even tried to keep up with me. I could get a little testy or whatever and instead of slinking off or pouting or getting all chest-poundy and testosterony like other guys, he'd keep on listening and talking. Also, he is easy on the eyes if you like your guys tall, blond, and blue-eyed. I think his ancestors were Vikings or something. He'd probably look good in a horned helmet. Which makes him the exact opposite of me with my curly hair and anorexic body. Not that I'm anorexic. I'm naturally extra slim. Fact is, I could use a few curves. My absurdly buxom mother tells me I'll grow into myself. Grow *into* myself? What, like a toenail? Sounds grotesque.

Even though we're from two different planets, Adam and I have a few things in common. Neither of us have any brothers or sisters, we are both lucky enough to have parents who are still alive and married, we live in nice houses, and we never go hungry. I guess you could say we're privileged, or at least not *under*privileged. We both plan to become rich and famous, and most important of all we have a similar sense of humor. Not many guys could make me laugh like Adam could.

But some of his faults are the size of the San Andreas.

Chapter Three
OBSESSION

Miz Fitz, Help!

A few months ago I slept with my boyfriend's best friend. It was just a one-time thing, but the guilt is killing me. Should I fess up?

— Guilty

Miz Fitz sez:

Keep your slutty mouth SHUT.

LITA

The clothes you wear on the first day of school can set the tone for that entire year. I had been thinking about it for weeks. It's not that I cared so much about fashion; it's just that clothes sort of define a person and it was our junior year, possibly the most important of our high school careers.

A few days before school started, I laid my clothes out on my bed, and Emily came over to inspect them.

"Black is always safe," she said, nodding at my black jeans and black cotton sweater.

"That's what I figured. But not too much of it. I don't want to turn into a Blair Thompson."

Emily laughed. "Now *there's* a girl with a serious fashion disability. All that makeup and leather and metal — is she trying to scare guys away?"

"Some guys think she's hot," I said.

"Yeah, guys with no taste."

Like Dennis, I thought to myself.

Emily held up one of my classic tees. "Tweety Bird?"

"For my retro-dork look," I said. Emily tossed it in the "maybe" pile, then went back to sorting through the pile on the foot of my bed. "You've got lots of earth tones. Very practical. A spot of color here and there . . . yellow socks?"

"Matches Tweety Bird, and they make me happy."

"Happy is good." She stood back and looked from me to the various piles of clothing. "I'd say you're in pretty good shape. Except maybe in the shoe department."

"I thought maybe we could hit the mall."

She looked at me. "You're counting on finding something at this late date?"

"I can always fall back on my clogs."

"Don't you dare wear those things again this year. You clomp like a Clydesdale."

"But they're *comfortable!*"

"Comfort is way overrated." She flopped across my bed, right on top of everything. Her light brown hair spread out around her head in a huge, spiky halo. I used to be horribly jealous of Emily's long, straight

13

hair, but that was before I decided to love myself for my curls. Now I only hate my hair about three days a week.

"You're wrinkling Tweety," I said.

"Tweety doesn't mind. God, I can hardly wait to see Dennis." She said this with a dreamy sigh. "You know, he spent the summer on the coast."

"It wasn't the whole summer. It was just three weeks. And it wasn't the coast, it was Lake Superior."

Emily stared up at the ceiling. "So Adam thought maybe Dennis liked me?"

"I told you last night. I asked him if Dennis was hot for your bod and he said, 'I don't know.'"

"Tell me his exact words again."

I was tempted to tattoo them on her forehead. "He said, 'I. Don't. Know.'"

"I wonder what he meant by that," said Emily.

You're pissing into the wind, I wanted to say. But of course I didn't. Emily was my best friend and keeping a best friend means knowing when to keep your mouth shut.

"Maybe you should write to Miz Fitz," I said. I was always telling people to read Miz Fitz.

"Are you kidding? Fitz is a total snark. Why should I write to her? Just to get publicly flamed on her stupid blog?"

Ouch. I took a moment to recover from that. I take remarks about Miz Fitz *very* personally.

"She just writes what she thinks," I said.

"Yeah, and she thinks everybody is an idiot."

"Everybody *is* an idiot. *Sometimes.*"

"I don't need reminding."

I wished Emily would meet some new guy to obsess over. Some guy who would like her back, for a change. But Emily would never pick a guy who might like her back. She was more into unrequited love.

"I have one class with Dennis this semester," she said. "Biology."

"I know that, Em. You've told me forty-seven times."

"Why forty-seven? Why not just jump up to fifty if you're going to exaggerate?"

"Forty-seven has a ring of authenticity about it."

Emily sighed again. "You are so lucky."

"How am I lucky?"

"You have Adam."

"I do? How so?"

"I mean, you have him as a backup. You know, for when you're between lovers."

"*Lovers?* I've never *had* a lover," I said.

"That is because you are too smart and too scary."

"How am I scary?"

"You take crap from no one." She turned her head to look at me. "Anyway, if you *did* have a lover, and then you broke up, you would have Adam to fall back on. He is, like, totally yours."

Adam and I had been friends forever, but not boyfriend-girlfriend friends. We are more like platonic buds, which is just as well because Adam has always had terrible taste in girlfriends. I'd seen three and one-third of them come and go, beginning with Gennifer Johanson, the most beautiful girl in the eighth grade. I don't know *exactly* what broke them up, but it might have had something to do with me telling Gennifer that Adam said she had fat cheeks.

Then there was Bridget Murphy back in the ninth grade, who made him buy her a necklace with his initials on it that she wore every day to school for six months. That wasn't embarrassing or anything. Ha! I think Adam was relieved when Bridget dumped him for the trivial but cute Frank Ness, who I strongly suspected of being a golden retriever disguised as a human. Bridget herself resembles a poodle, and they made an amazingly cute couple, as I pointed out to Bridget on numerous occasions. Arf arf!

The abominable Tracy Spink, better known as Spacy Tracy, came along a year later. Fortunately, for the fate of the children they will never have, Adam came to his senses and dumped Tracy when she confessed to him that she hated Buddy Holly.

Okay, so Adam was a little weird about Buddy Holly, who's been dead for more than half a century. I told Tracy that Buddy was a second-rate musician who'd had the good fortune to die before people figured out how lame he really was, and I suggested that it was her job to make Adam see the light. Now, *I* know better than to say anything negative about Buddy to Adam. Tracy, well, she was never the brightest LED in the display.

The "one-third girlfriend" was Ashley Strickland, who set her sights on Adam around the time he gave Spacy Tracy the heave-ho. I observed Ashley's technique carefully as I am quite interested in human mating behavior. Mostly it involved touching her hair, laughing at everything Adam said, and finding excuses to sort of bump up against him like a hungry cat. Was it working? Hard to say. Adam seemed only marginally aware of her giggles and bumps. I, of course, understood from the get-go that they were entirely wrong for each other.

Anyway, Ashley went to the East Coast for the summer with her parents, and when she returned she announced to anyone who would listen that she had a new boyfriend in the form of a clam digger from Long Island. She never really got started with Adam, hence the "one-third girlfriend" rating. I didn't have to do a thing. But I was monitoring the situation.

Clearly, Adam had some desirable qualities or he wouldn't have attracted three and one-third girlfriends in four years. He had a wide-open face and a smile that makes some girls go all blushy and blinky-eyed, but he wasn't so good at picking them.

I, however, have excellent taste.

"What are you thinking about?" Emily asked.

I laughed. "The utterly insupportable concept of Adam being my backup guy. I told you what happened the time we tried to make out."

"Oh yeah — the famous giggle fest."

"Exactly. Every time he tried to kiss me, I burst out laughing, and then he started laughing, too. It's like we're *friends*, but there's no *chemistry*. Frankly, I don't think Adam is that interested in girls."

"You think he's gay?"

"I think he gets turned on by wheeling and dealing. He's a *business*-sexual."

"There is such a thing?"

"There must be. Where do you think little businesses come from?"

"Ewww!"

"Anyway, Adam and I, we just know each other too well. Besides, you know I go for the dark-haired, fiery-eyed, mysterious type."

"What type do you think Adam goes for?"

"I'm thinking skankish. But I'm really not sure."

"But you know him better than anybody!"

It was true. I knew Adam the way I knew my own reflection. Still, hardly a day went by when he didn't find some way to surprise me.

Chapter Four
NAKED, THROBBING LUST

Hi, Miz Fitz,

I am sort of nerdy and most of my friends are nerds or geeks, too, but this one guy I really really like is not nerdy at all. Do not-nerdy boys ever go for nerdy girls? Do I need a makeover?

— Nerdilicious

Miz Fitz sez:

Makeovers are way overrated. Eventually, you always slump back to the person you used to be. I suggest you find this guy's inner nerd. All boys have one.

ADAM

Dennis Long said, "Do I have bad breath?"

I leaned away from him and made gagging noises.

His forehead crumpled. I laughed.

We were sitting on a bench at the Mall of America, better known as the Megamall, still working on the ultra-colossal bucket of popcorn Dennis had bought at the movie theater.

"Your breath is fine," I said. "A little popcorny maybe, but not like something died in your mouth."

Dennis ate another handful of popcorn, thinking hard. I could tell he was thinking because he got that look like his face hurt.

"Is it because I'm fat?"

"You're not fat. You're beefy."

"*Beefy?*"

"Solid. Well built. Powerful."

"Like a cow."

"Like a *bull*."

"Maybe I should've got unbuttered popcorn."

"Seriously, you're not fat."

"Is it because I'm Asian?"

I snorted. "Why would you think that? Have you even tried to talk to her?"

"Three times. I said hello to her, and she completely ignored me."

"Where was that?"

"Last April, at school. About a week after she moved here. She was talking to Bree Feider and Yola Garfield, and I walked right up to them and said hi, and nothing happened."

"What did you expect to happen?"

"Like, hi back?"

"Bree and Yolanda don't talk to anybody who doesn't score a nine-plus on their cool-o-meter."

"I wasn't talking to them, I was talking to Blair."

"Blair was probably just trying to break into the Bree Feider clique."

"The second time was in June. I saw her at the mall with Chelsea and, sort of, you know, nodded at her as they walked by."

"Maybe she didn't recognize you."

"Exactly! 'Cause I'm Chinese."

I rolled my eyes. "What about the third time?"

"Last week." He closed his eyes and winced. "At the zoo."

"What were you doing at the *zoo*?"

"I took Sean." Sean was Dennis's little brother. "Sean likes to watch the monkeys."

"What was *Blair* doing at the zoo?"

"She was working there. At the Dairy Queen. I bought a couple of dip cones from her. I told her I liked her hat."

"What hat?"

"A little Dairy Queen hat. It looked cute on her."

"You are hopeless," I said, laughing. "What did she say?"

"She said, 'Next!'"

"Ouch."

"I know." He picked an old maid from the bottom of the popcorn bucket and crunched it between his molars.

"I think you need a book about what girls want," I said, thinking again about my book idea.

"What book is that?"

"The bestseller I'm going to write."

"Yeah, *right*. I'll tell you what I need. I need Blair."

"So why don't you just ask her out? Get it over with."

Dennis looked at me. "Are you out of your mind?" He crunched another old maid.

"You're gonna bust a tooth doing that," said a voice right behind us.

I tipped my head back and looked into Lita Wold's upside-down face. "Hey, Leet."

"Name's not Leet," said Lita.

"Hey, Emily," I said, spotting Emily hiding behind Lita. But Emily was so blinded by Dennis's magnificence that I might as well have been talking to the air.

LITA

Adam Merchant and Dennis Long made an odd-looking pair: the Cheerful Viking and the Mysterious Asian. I could see what Emily liked about Dennis. Those dark eyes, long lashes, and full lips had a certain appeal. She was looking at him so hard I was afraid she'd injure herself.

"Shoe shopping, huh?" Adam said, looking at the boxes dangling from our hands.

"We got a little deranged," I said.

"I'll be returning mine tomorrow," Emily said.

"Why buy them if you're just going to take them back?" Dennis asked.

Emily froze up. I jumped in to save her, the way I always do.

"It's *shopping*, Einstein."

Dennis didn't get it.

"We are girls. We shop. It's all about process."

Dennis absorbed that, then said, "But since you've already enjoyed the shopping *process*, wouldn't it be easier to return the shoes now, and save yourself the trouble of coming back tomorrow?"

I looked at Emily again. "Girls are from Earth, boys are from Bogzillia," I said.

"Maybe we *should* return the shoes," Emily said, staring at Dennis in a way any male other than Dennis would have instantly recognized as naked, throbbing lust.

I grabbed Adam's hand and pulled him to his feet and said, "Come, Bogzillian creature, I wish to show you an article of clothing you just have to own."

"I don't need an article of clothing," he said.

"Yes, you do." I dragged him off, leaving Emily and Dennis staring after us.

ADAM

"I don't know if that was such a good idea," I said to Lita.

"It can't hurt," Lita said, looking back at Dennis and Emily. "Maybe they'll, you know, *talk*."

"I doubt it. Dennis will probably say something incredibly stupid —"

"— and Emily will obsess over it endlessly, and Dennis will be clueless, and when we get back they'll both be flailing about in a state of bewilderment and unfulfilled sexual desire."

"That's what I was going to say."

"No, it isn't."

"So why leave them flailing?"

"They need the practice." Lita stopped walking. "Here's your new sweater."

We were standing at the entrance to The Gulch, the latest money pit for the fashion dependent. The sweater display was right there — stacks of nubbly, black cotton things with tiny multicolor polka dots. One of the salesclerks, a scrawny black-haired guy with a pointy nose, said to me, "You'd look fantastic in one of these. It's our hottest new item."

"So, if I buy one and wear it to school Monday, there'll be, like, forty other guys wearing the same polka-dot sweater?"

The sales guy frowned. "We haven't actually sold *that* many. . . ."

I didn't buy the sweater.

"It would have looked nerdilicious on you," Lita said as we left the store.

"I don't need a sweater. Besides, I'm saving my money for my new venture."

"You and your ventures." Lita looked back at the forlorn sales drone. "He was cute," she said.

"Your type," I said. "Dark and pointy-nosed."

"That's dark and *fiery eyed*!"

"My mistake."

When we got back to the bench where we'd left Dennis and Emily, they were both gone.

"Maybe they went to get something to eat," Lita said.

We took an escalator up to the food court and made our way through the ring of fast-food joints. It was like running an obstacle course: Cinnabon, Sbarro, BK, Mrs. Fields — one great smell after another.

We found Dennis eating a giant bag of chocolate chip cookies, all by himself.

"Where's Emily?" Lita asked.

Dennis shrugged. "I think she's, like, got PMS or something."

Lita gave Dennis a scathing look. I thought things were going to get ugly, but she pulled out her cell and thumbed in a number. "Em. Where are you?" I heard her say as she walked off.

I sat down and grabbed a cookie.

"So what happened?" I asked.

"Well, we went to return those shoes she bought that she wasn't going to keep, and we were talking — I don't even know what about — and all of a sudden she looks like she's gonna start crying or something, and she takes off." He shrugged. "So I thought I'd come up here for a cookie."

"What did you say to her?"

"I don't *know*. We were talking about shoes. Hey —" He interrupted himself by stuffing another cookie in his face. I waited for him to chew and swallow. "What do you think a girl would do if a guy bought her a nice pair of shoes?"

"I suppose it would depend on the shoes," I said.

"A really *nice* pair of shoes."

"I — wait a sec — who are we talking about here . . . uh-oh. Not *Blair!*"

"It was just a thought," he said.

I found Emily on the other side of the food court picking at a tray of French fries.

"Are you okay?" I asked.

"I'm in wretchedness," she said. "I am the most pitiful of the piteous." She held up a French fry between her thumb and forefinger. It sagged listlessly. "I am the human version of this French fry." She dropped the fry on the tray, and wiped her hand on a napkin.

"What happened?"

"He doesn't know I exist."

"Just because Dennis is blind doesn't mean you're invisible."

"We get to the shoe store and I'm returning my shoes and he's like, 'Check out these high heels,' and he asks me to try them on, so I get the sales guy to bring out a pair of sevens and I put them on and he says, 'Wow, those are great!' And I'm thinking maybe I should buy them — even though I never *ever* wear heels — because I like the way he's looking at my feet. Then he says, 'Do you know Blair Thompson?' and I'm like, *Excuse* me? And he says, 'I wonder what size shoe she wears.'"

Emily picked up another fry, tore it in half, and dropped it onto the tray.

"So then I say, 'Why do you want to know *that*?' and he says, 'I was just thinking those shoes would look good on her.'"

"You should have brought one of those heels down on his foot."

"See what I mean? You're *scary*. That's why you don't have a boyfriend."

"How did we start talking about *my* pathetic love life?" I said.

Emily shrugged and returned to her lament. "So then — this is how unbelievably pitiful I am — I tell Dennis to get lost . . ."

"A natural reaction."

". . . then I go back in the store and buy them." She gave me a defiant look.

"You bought the shoes?" I said.

Emily leaned back, lifted her leg, and plonked one high-heeled foot right next to the tray of mangled fries.

"Holy Gaga," I said.

Chapter Five
HISTORY LESSON

Miz, you are the BEST!!!!! How old are you? Do you always follow your heart?
— *Curious*

Miz Fitz sez:
I am ninety-seven years old. I follow no one.

LITA

When I got home, my mother was all over me because I'd left a mess in the kitchen and I hadn't cleaned the bathroom and about six other things I'd done or not done. She gets like that when she's in what she calls the "sticky middle" of a novel.

My mother is the semi-famous Amanda Maize, author of more than sixty paperback romance novels. I've never understood how this could be, as she is about the most unromantic person I've ever met. But you should read her books. They're hot. I think she must use writing to exercise — and I mean *exercise*, not *exorcize* — her demons. I should know because I do it, too.

Anyway, when she gets to the "sticky middle," she frequently leaves her desk to stalk the house searching for reasons to criticize me or my dad. I think that's why my dad travels so much.

I cleaned for twenty minutes but as soon as I heard my mother back in her den rattling her keyboard, I tiptoed up to my room to exercise my own demons. In other words, I logged in and checked Miz Fitz for new questions. There were three.

One girl wrote to say that her little brother was always jumping out and scaring her. She wanted to know what she could do to stop him.

I thought for a moment, then wrote and posted this response:

> Miz Fitz sez:
> He does that because he is a boy. Boys like to hear girls scream. Try fake crying. Boys hate it when girls cry. If that doesn't work, nail him with your pepper spray.

There you have it. My Big Secret. A Secret then known only to me, *moi*, and I. Lita Wold is the secret identity of infamous power blogger Miz Fitz, who says all the snarky, pissy, nasty, brutally honest, demonic things that I am forced to repress in real life. Miz Fitz is Mr. Hyde to my Dr. Jekyll. My Darth Vader, as it were. People write to me, and I let them have it. Funny thing, though — they keep coming back for more. Some people thrive on abuse. It's almost as if they want Miz Fitz to spank them. For example:

> *Dear Miz Fitz,*
> *My current relationship with my BF sux beyond the farthest reaches of suxdom. Dumping him is a no-brainer, but should I find*

another BF first or dump him now before hooking up with another guy? I have several who are interested.

— *GorgeousGirl*

Miz Fitz sez:

Wow, you must be really amazing. How will you ever find a guy who thinks you're as great as you do?

The meaner and more sarcastic I got, the more people posted questions, which was the opposite of real life. If I'd said something like that to Bree Feider for example, there would be consequences.

Of course, Miz Fitz also offered kind, useful advice:

O Wondrous Miz Fitz,

I am not the most attractive girl in my school. In fact, I am not even the 200th most attractive girl. And there are only like 223 of us. When I look at myself in the mirror I want to die.

— *Ugly Betty*

Miz Fitz sez:

Look up the high school yearbook pictures of future rock stars. It will help.

Occasionally, I made up my own questions. Like this one, which I hoped Emily would read:

My Dear Miz Fitz, Wisest of the Wise,

I am totally completely in love with a guy who thinks I'm lawn furniture. How can I get his attention?
— Moonstruck

Miz Fitz sez:

There are many solutions to your problem, but they are unreliable and (in certain cases) illegal. I recommend transferring your love vibe to

"Lita!"

My mother, summoning me. I ignored her. Sometimes she gives up.

another more deserving male. Find one who has money and

"Lydia!"

make sure he smells good.

Maybe Emily would read it.

"Lydia Wold!"

I shoved back from my desk, opened my door, and shouted down the stairs.

"What?"

"Come down here!"

I found the semi-famous Amanda Maize standing in front of the kitchen sink, staring down at a dishcloth draped over the front edge.

That's right. One wet, slightly drippy scrap of blue fabric was the source of all the screaming.

"What," my mother said, pointing one slightly crooked finger at the dishcloth, "is that?"

"That," I said, "is a dishrag. Is there anything else I can help you with?"

I realized as I spoke that I was still in Miz Fitz mode.

"I *know* what it *is*," my mother said. "I want to know why it is hanging all sopping wet on the edge of the sink, dripping down the front of the cabinet and onto the floor, which I mopped this morning while you were off playing with your friends at the mall."

"I wasn't playing. I was shopping."

"*This*," said my mother, stabbing her finger at the dishcloth, "does not belong on the edge of the sink. Please remove it."

You might think that my mother was some sort of neat freak, but you would be wrong. It was only when she was having trouble writing one of her books that she suddenly got all OCD and did things like cleaning the peephole in the front door and arranging the linens by color and nitpicking every single move I made. The fact that these moods only lasted a week or two made them no less irritating.

I picked up the dishcloth, wrung it out, and hung it on the rack behind the cabinet door. "There. Are you happy now?"

"Ecstatic," said my mother, loading her voice with a triple dose of sarcasm.

"It would have been easier if you'd just done it yourself," I said, knowing the moment the words left my mouth that in about twenty seconds we were going to be screaming at each other.

"Oh, *really*," she said. "And I suppose I should devote my life to following you around, cleaning up your messes?"

"My messes? I'm neater than you are. Look at your —"

"Don't you talk to me that way! I —"

We went at it. The semi-famous Amanda Maize started crying when I said the reason Dad was always on the road was because she was such a nag, and I immediately felt so bad that the only thing I could do was get even madder than I was to start with, which led to some accusations about treating her family like characters in some crappy romance novel, and . . . You get the picture. It only lasted about three minutes before I slammed out of the house for an Anonymous Anger Walk, walking fast down Holden Avenue, where I was pretty sure I wouldn't run into anybody I knew. I contemplated stowing away on a Paris-bound 747 because in Paris you eat in cafés and don't have to clean up after yourself or deal with your deranged mother. Unless you are French — I suppose they have crazy mothers, too.

I was walking quickly, staring into space while sipping imaginary espresso near an imaginary Eiffel Tower, when I practically tripped over a pair of legs sticking out onto the sidewalk. The rest of the body was underneath the front end of an old, gray convertible parked in a driveway.

I said, "Hey, you're obstructing traffic!"

The guy slid out from under the car and looked up at me. He was as dark and fiery eyed as they come. A little greasy, though.

"Hey," he said.

"Hey yourself. You almost tripped me." I can be very not-charming when I am in Anger Walk mode.

He sat up and gestured at the car, which looked as if it hadn't moved in a long time. Both headlights were missing, and the body was splotchy with gray primer. "Think I should put up some orange cones?"

"Why don't you just call a wrecker?" I said.

"Wrecker? This is a sixty-nine GTO! A classic!"

"Classically dorky, maybe." I wondered why I'd never seen him around school. Maybe he'd just moved here. More likely, he was a dropout.

"You wait and see." He grinned. "I get her pimped, you'll beg me for a ride."

"Yeah, right." I made up a new rule on the spot: Never ride with a guy who calls his car *her*.

"You go to Wellstone?" he asked.

"Harvard," I said. I was not about to tell this dropout car jockey anything even remotely true.

"Yeah, right." He stood and wiped his greasy hands on his greasy jeans. His gray tank top was spotted with oils stains and smears. He had a nice, lanky body, though, with great shoulders. "What's your name?"

"Emma Woodhouse," I said, naming one of my favorite Jane Austen characters.

"Pleased to meet you, Emma Woodhouse." He thrust out a hand. "I'm Brett Andrews."

I looked at his grease-darkened hand.

"Sorry," he said, pulling it back. "Guess I'm a little grungy. Putting in a new starter."

"Maybe then you'll be able to get your car off the sidewalk."

"It's not actually *on* the sidewalk."

I had a sudden, overwhelming urge to get away. I was starting to like him, and the last thing I needed was some grease-monkey dropout in my life. I started walking.

"See you later, Emma Woodhouse," he said.

"I can hardly wait," I replied over my shoulder, giving the words a sarcastic spin. Somehow I had felt that getting in that last word was important. I kept on walking and wondering if he thought I was a total bitch — or maybe he thought I was sassy and spunky. If he was even thinking about me at all. Not that it mattered, because there was no way I cared what some retro grease-monkey dropout thought, even if he was flat out the best-looking guy I'd seen, well, *ever.*

Chapter Six
VIAGRA AND BAZOOKAS

Miz Fitz,

Why are boys obsessed with breasts?

— A Cup

Miz Fitz sez:

Boys are mostly obsessed with themselves. However, it is true that guys can't help gawking at cleavage. They like looking at monster trucks, too. That doesn't mean they want one in their driveway.

ADAM

That first day of school you think everything is possible. Classes will be easier, everybody will think you're cool, and the girl of your dreams will slip a nude photo of herself into your locker. . . .

Only this was what I found in my locker:

TO ALL STUDENTS:

A POLICY OF RANDOM WEEKLY LOCKER CHECKS WILL GO INTO EFFECT THIS YEAR. ALL LOCKERS MUST BE CLEAN, ORDERLY, UNMARKED BY GRAFFITI, STICKERS, OR OTHER UNAUTHORIZED DEFACEMENT, AND FREE OF UNAPPROVED ITEMS INCLUDING:

- •DRUGS (UNLESS PRESCRIBED)
- •WEAPONS
- •UNWASHED ATHLETIC WEAR
- •NOISEMAKING DEVICES (AIR HORNS, AMPLIFIED MUSIC DEVICES, ETC.)

UNAPPROVED ITEMS NOT APPROVED MUST BE APPROVED BY ADMINISTRATION.

ADRIAN GRAVES, PRINCIPAL

Bob Glaus, two lockers down, was looking at his own copy of the note. He said, "Does this mean I have to leave my bazooka at home?"

"Not if you can get Graves to approve your unapproved not approved item."

Just then, Blair Thompson came sashaying down the hall. Bob and I stared.

"I change my rating to nine point seven," Bob said. "Check out *those* bazookas."

He was right. Blair had definitely cranked up the skank-o-meter since last spring. First, you should know that Blair Thompson was *built*. She had a front end like a pair of cruise missiles and legs that, as my grandfather would say, reached all the way to the ground — we could see practically every inch of them below that black faux-leather miniskirt.

Miniskirt, you ask? *Nobody* wears miniskirts at Wellstone High — let alone the fake-leather variety. Nobody but Blair Thompson, that is. And those cruise missiles I mentioned? They were about to blow out the semi-sheer black-lace top she'd somehow managed to squeeze them into.

Top all that off with a layer of makeup that included several ounces of black eye shadow, a slab of bloodred lipstick, matching nails, a waterfall of red-streaked black hair, and — you get the picture. I might have to devote an entire chapter of my book to what boys think of makeup.

"Skank-o-freaking-*rama,*" Bob said.

"I think she's permanently disqualified herself from membership in the Bree Feider crowd," I said. But I was thinking that, skanky or not, Blair walked down that hallway like she owned it. I couldn't imagine her giving a bunny turd about what Bree Feider thought.

"They disqualified her a long time ago, when Bree found out that Blair's mom worked at Fleet Farm."

"That sounds totally Bree-like."

"I wonder why she dresses that way."

"She probably wonders the same thing about you," I said.

"Who, me?" Bob looked down at his new, nubbly, black cotton sweater with little multicolor polka dots. "What's wrong with the way I dress?"

LITA

On the way into school I asked Emily if she'd read Miz Fitz recently.

"I told you," Emily said, "I don't *like* Miz Fitz."

"If her advice is good, what's the difference if you like her?"

"I don't need good advice. I need Dennis."

Which is why I was in the library between first and second period printing out hard copy of the latest Miz Fitz blog entries for Emily. I'd force it down her throat if I had to. But wouldn't you know it, Mrs. Corinna Crowe's pink-nailed fingers came over my shoulder and snatched the first page right out of my hands.

"That's enough, Lita," said Mrs. Crowe (aka the Evil Librarian). Her prim, smug voice had grown even primmer and smugger over the summer. "Just because it's a new school year does not mean you can make free and easy with school printers." She grabbed the second page as it emerged from the printer. "Principal Graves has made it quite clear — there will be no yellow journalism tolerated in this school. We have our own school newspaper. If you must read sensationalistic drivel such as this" — crumpling the paper in her fist — "print it out at home."

"My printer's out of ink."

Mrs. Crowe's tiny nostrils flared. "Be that as it may, I will not have you reading this trash in this library."

Miss Morris (aka the Good Librarian) was listening from her perch behind the desk. She caught my eye and gave me a wink.

"What ever happened to freedom of speech?" I said to Mrs. Crowe.

She made a whistling sound through her nose and stalked off.

From the way I've described her you might think that Mrs. Crowe was about six hundred years old with snaggleteeth and *Tyrannosaurus* breath, but you would be wrong. Mrs. Corinna Crowe was in her late twenties, quite pretty, and relatively fragrant in the breath department. Also, she had a voluptuous figure that her conservative clothing could not hope to hide. The few boys who hung out in the library spent more time staring at Mrs. Crowe than they did reading. But Mrs. Crowe's looks were completely canceled out by the fact that she was a hard-core, hyper-conservative prude. Last year she and two of the school board members tried to ban Judy Blume's novel *Forever*. Miss Morris and the entire Language Arts department stood up to them, and the matter was dropped. However, I noticed that ever since, *Forever* always seems to be out on loan. I suspected that Mrs. Crowe "borrowed" it herself to make sure nobody else could read it.

Our other librarian, Miss Morris, was totally cool — though you wouldn't think it to look at her. She was fifty-some years old, chunky, frowny, frizzy, blinky, twitchy, and a fashion disaster. I didn't know where she bought her clothes and hoped to never find out. Ditto her haircut, which looked like someone had upended a mixing bowl on her head and used the rim as a cutting guide. But in all the places it really counted, Miss Morris was completely awesome. Get her started on First Amendment rights and she could scare the trunk off an elephant.

Miss Morris might have looked the other way if she'd seen me printing out Miz Fitz, but technically Mrs. Crowe was right about the school rules: To the Powers That Be at Wellstone High School, Miz Fitz's blog was about as welcome as a porn site.

So far, I had been able to keep Miz Fitz's identity a secret — but it was well known that *someone* connected with Wellstone High was behind the blog. Why? Because I had run a piece the previous April called "Trashy Teachers: The First Annual Wellstone Faculty Trash Survey" in which I explored the contents of selected faculty home garbage cans. The results were, shall we say, revealing, particularly with regard to Mrs. Crowe, whose trash revealed, among other things, two empty Ex-Lax boxes and a nearly full prescription bottle of Viagra.

You can draw your own conclusions from that, but no matter what you come up with, things did not look so good for *Mr.* Crowe.

Chapter Seven
SPEAKING BOGZILLIAN

Miz Fitz,

This guy in my history class creeps me out with his staring. What would you do?

— Ogled

Miz Fitz sez:

Creepy oglers demand extreme measures. You could wear a burka, but a more elegant solution might be to threaten to remove his eyeballs with your fingernails.

ADAM

I was making a list of topics for the book when Dennis and Bob plopped down on either side of me. Bob's tray was loaded with three squares of school pizza and a bowl of what I hoped was banana pudding because if it wasn't banana pudding I didn't want to think about it. Dennis, no doubt trying to make up for yesterday's cookies, had made himself a pile of greenery from the salad bar — then loaded it with about a thousand calories of ranch dressing.

Me, I was gnawing on beef jerky, with a square of chocolate cake on deck.

"Whatcha doon?" Bob asked through a mouthful of pizza.

"Working on a new idea," I said.

"Another Rent-A-Teen?"

"No," I said, thinking back to my failed business from three months earlier. The idea of Rent-A-Teen was that I would hook up teens with homeowners who needed work done — babysitting, lawn mowing, garage cleaning, you name it — but here's what happened: About half the kids I talked to said, "Sure, I guess, if, you know, like, I got nothing else going on. I mean, if the money's good." At the time, that sounded to me like a big YES.

And the homeowners I talked to mostly liked the idea, and promised to get in touch the next time they needed help with a project.

I got one call that week. Mr. Gillespie needed his back shed cleaned out. "Shouldn't take but half an hour," he said.

"No problem, we can do that job for our minimum fee of fifteen dollars," I said. "I'll have somebody there this afternoon."

My first call was to Bob, who had been among my most enthusiastic recruits. But Bob had something else planned. Ten calls later I was scratching my head over how unbelievably *busy* everybody was. Or lazy. It was after noon when I gave up. Even though I had envisioned myself in a strictly managerial position, I decided I would have to do the job myself.

Mr. Gillespie's "shed" was more like a two-car garage. It took me four hours to clean it out. When I was finished, filthy and exhausted, I presented my bill: four hours at fifteen bucks an hour.

"Whoa there, son, you told me fifteen dollars!"

"Yeah, but you told me it was a half-hour job!"

"Can I help it if you're slow?"

Slow? I'd worked like a demon. But Mr. Gillespie would not hear of it. I took the fifteen bucks and headed for home.

Rent-A-Teen's second call was from Mrs. Kaufman, who desperately needed someone to babysit her three kids while she did some shopping and got a haircut. I carefully explained our rates to her, emphasizing our *fifteen-dollars-per-hour* policy.

"Of course, dear," she said. "Can you have someone here by two this afternoon?"

I got lucky on the third call and lined up Brianna Blackmun. The only catch was that I had to drive her over to the Kaufmans', then give her a ride home later.

Fortunately, my mom let me use the car, and everything went according to plan — until I returned to pick up Brianna after the job.

She looked *terrible.*

She had a bruise on her forehead, and her eyes were puffy from crying.

"It was awful," she said, throwing herself into the passenger seat of my mother's Corolla. "One of them hit me with a *broom!*"

"Really? The seven-year-old?"

"The middle one. She was the worst."

"You got beat up by a five-year-old girl?"

Brianna gave me a narrow-eyed look and crossed her arms. "It wasn't worth it," she said. "Sixty dollars for four hours in hell."

I waited till we got to her house and she was climbing out of the car to remind her that twenty percent of the sixty dollars she'd earned was my commission.

She looked in at me, laughed, and slammed the door. That was the end of Rent-A-Teen.

"This idea is way better than Rent-A-Teen," I told Bob. "I'm writing a book."

Blair Thompson walked by. We stopped talking to watch her until she disappeared at the back of the lunchroom.

Dennis shoved a huge forkful of salad into his mouth and said, "Yaroobligebuke?"

"Sorry, I don't speak Bogzillian," I said, stealing Lita's favorite made-up word.

He swallowed. "You're really writing a *book*? I thought you were kidding."

"Serious," I said, "I'm writing a book about how boys and girls really think."

Dennis laughed. "Yeah, right."

That kind of bugged me. I mean, I was never as good a student as Dennis — not even close — but I knew how to get things done. When I get obsessive, I am unstoppable. Dennis, on the other hand, is scary smart, but he couldn't even bring himself to ask Blair Thompson out on a date.

"I'm totally serious," I said. And as the words left my mouth, I really and truly knew for the first time that I was really going to do it.

All I had to do was write the thing.

LITA

I found Emily sitting alone at the back of the lunchroom stirring a cup of mango yogurt.

"How are the new shoes working out?" I asked.

She shrugged listlessly. "I saw Dennis this morning. I don't think he noticed."

"First day of school. He's probably distracted."

"Yeah, distracted by Blair Thompson."

"She's hard not to look at, what with all the skank vibes she's sending out." I peeled the top back from my own yogurt cup and spooned some cherry-vanilla wonderfulness into my mouth.

Emily said, "It's not her skankiness I object to, it's her fashion sense."

"I think those two qualities are intimately connected. Like sweat and stink."

"I just wish she'd quit flirting with Dennis."

"Flirting?" I said.

"You know. Walking where he can see her."

"I don't think she's flirting, exactly. Unless you mean she's flirting with the entire male population."

"*Exactly*," said Emily.

I tried to change the subject. "Ever wonder how come all the really cute guys are obsessed with sports, or gay, or covered with grease? I met one of the latter yesterday crawling out from under a car."

"Why were you under a car?"

"*He* was the one under the car."

"And he was cute?"

"Majorly," I said. "But a little greasy."

"Maybe he cleans up nice."

"Ha!" I said. I'd been thinking the exact same thing.

ADAM

If you want to get rich it helps to have a degree from someplace like Harvard Business School. And if you want to study business it helps to know math so you can count all your money. And if you want to have a strong background in math, you gotta take calculus.

That was how I ended up in Mr. Sklansky's class, fifth period, on the west side of the building. You'd think a guy smart enough to teach calculus would know better than to schedule his class right after lunch with afternoon sun pouring through the window. Staying awake was going to be tough. I looked over the available seats. If I sat right in front I'd be more likely to stay awake, but I would also be within range of Sklansky's infamous shotgun spittle. I noticed a couple of empty seats next to Dennis, right in the middle of the room.

"Hey," I said, taking the seat to his left.

He looked at me. "Adam? *You're* taking calculus?"

"You don't think I'm up to it?"

Dennis shrugged. "You hated trig."

"I'd rather take this now than later. Get it over with."

"I guess. I —" Just like *that*, his face went slack.

"You okay?" I asked.

He was staring at something on the other side of me, his mouth hanging open. I turned to look and my jaw dropped, too.

Blair Thompson was taking the desk immediately to my left.

Blair Thompson? Calculus? What *planet* was this?

I watched her take out her new calculus text and a black hardcover notebook. She positioned them neatly on her desk. Unlike the rest of the students, who were slumped, sprawled, or half melted with after-lunch lethargy, Blair seemed eager to get on with the learning process. She unclipped a mechanical pencil from the spine of her notebook, clicked it, and began copying the lesson plan for the semester from the board. She had remarkably neat handwriting.

At one point, as I watched her write, she turned her head and looked straight at me and I noticed for the first time that her irises were an odd shade of brown flecked with streaks of green. She smiled, showing me teeth that were so even you just knew she'd had a mouthful of braces in the eighth grade.

I looked away, feeling my face grow warm. What was *that* about? I have never been a blusher, and looking people in the eye was something I did all the time, but for some reason I was embarrassed to be caught gawking.

To cover, I kept turning my head until I was looking at Dennis, who was now sitting ramrod straight, sucking his gut against his spine, staring straight ahead at the blackboard — I guess just in case Blair accidentally looked at him, so she would see what a well-built, attentive student he was.

And I was sitting directly between the two of them. No problem staying awake in *this* class.

Chapter Eight
THE INVISIBLE HAT

Hey, Miz Fitz,

This guy I've been seeing leaves his mouth hanging open all the time. It makes him look stupid. Have you ever had that problem?

— Doreen

Miz Fitz sez:

Unless you believe he is openmouthed due to your stunning beauty, you have a serious problem. Try superglue.

LITA

Emily and I decided to walk home from school because it was a gorgeous end-of-summer day. And because the bus would be *teeming* with smelly ninth and tenth graders. And because nobody had offered us a ride.

But it really *was* a beautiful day, all bright and sunny with just a hint of early September crispness in the air. Emily had cheered up somewhat and was excited about her new art teacher, Ms. Janko, a cigarette-smoking lesbian biker who, on the very first day of class, had uttered the word *bullshit*.

"What was she talking about?" I asked.

"She was telling us her classroom rules. One of them was 'Don't give me any bullcrap.'"

"Bull*crap*?"

"You could tell she meant bull*shit*."

"How do you know she's a lesbian?"

"She has man hair. And she wears a rainbow pin."

"That is so incredibly uncool, it is almost cool. I'm going to dump trig and transfer to art class!"

"Seriously?"

"Maybe, maybe not." Since my art aptitude was off the scale (on the low end) it would probably be "not."

"Maybe I should move to New York and become a famous painter," Emily said.

"I thought you were going to be a fashion designer."

"I'll do both. Marry a movie star, make a billion dollars, and die happy the day before my fortieth birthday."

"You might want to wait till you're fifty. All that money, you'll be able to afford some wicked plastic surgery."

It was fun. We had been walking and talking for an entire three minutes without one single mention of Dennis Long. I told Emily I'd had another fight with my mom.

"The usual nuclear exchange?"

"Pretty much. Over a dishrag. Of course, later on, when I got back home we both acted like it never happened."

"I guess that beats days of sulking, like we do at my house." Emily stopped walking and stared across the street.

"What is it?" I asked.

"Must. Have. Sustenance," she said, pointing at Fratellone's Bakery.

I am always up for a bakery experience.

Fratellone's was an old-fashioned no-frills bakery: no espresso, no gourmet jelly beans, no sandwiches, no Wi-Fi. Just baked goods. But they had a couple of tables out front under the awning where a couple of famished young ladies could sit and delicately scarf carbs.

I was on my second raised, glazed doughnut with multicolor sprinkles, and Emily was making her way through an enormous bear claw when an old, gray convertible with two missing headlights rumbled up to the curb. I gave Emily a kick under the table.

"Check him out," I said. She looked over as grease-monkey dreamboat Brett Andrews climbed out of the car.

"Afternoon, ladies," he said, tipping an imaginary hat as he walked past us into the bakery. I could have sworn he was wearing the exact same filthy tank top as before.

Emily and I looked at each other, our eyes wide. She tipped her own imaginary hat, lowered her voice as far as it would go, and said, "Afternoon, ladies." We burst out laughing — me with a mouthful of doughnut — and I got sprinkles up my nose. When Brett came back out with his bag full of whatever, I was coughing and snorting into my napkin.

Once again he tipped an imaginary hat. I thought Emily's face would shatter, she was trying so hard to keep from laughing, and after that all I could think about was the sprinkles burning my sinuses and that I hoped to God he hadn't recognized me.

We watched him drive off.

"Was that *him*?" Emily asked.

"The greasy car guy, yeah. His name is Brett."

"He's almost as cute as Dennis." She sighed, and her eyes fogged up.

I sighed, too, thinking that compared to Brett, Dennis was a peanut.

ADAM

After school I took the bus to the downtown library to find a book about how to get published. Turned out there was a whole shelf of books about nothing else. I grabbed an armful and dug in.

Not the funnest reading I've ever done. After paging through the first few books I noticed that they all pretty much said the same thing: First you write a book, then you find a literary agent, then the agent finds a publisher, and shortly thereafter your book is being sold at bookstores across the country. None of the books really said how long that process would take. It could be months.

It seemed like a lot of work — then it hit me. Why bother with agents and publishers when I could just write the book and get a few hundred copies printed? I could sell them myself and keep all the money. But how would I get the money to pay for having the books printed? It only took about three seconds for me to work that one out: I'd *presell* the book.

A few minutes later, I was flipping through a book called *Publish Yourself!* when I noticed a familiar figure perusing the stacks. It was the incredibly hot Mrs. Corinna Crowe, who has done more to increase the number of guys using the school library than Harry Potter and Stephen King combined.

She seemed to be intent on one particular section of one shelf. I watched as she pulled out one book after another, flipped quickly through each of them, and put them back on the shelf with librarian precision.

Mrs. Crowe was not wearing her usual school librarian outfit. She had changed from her trademark skirt into tight jeans and a pink T-shirt with an upside-down Nike logo on the front. I was admiring the way she filled it out when she turned and I saw the back of the T-shirt.

Just DON'T Do It!

✓ No Sex	✓ No Drugs
✓ No Alcohol	✓ No Tobacco
✓ No Tattoos	✓ No Gay Marriage
✓ No Abortion	✓ No Body Piercing

That's a lot of *NO* for one lousy pink T-shirt. I buried my face in *Publish Yourself!* so she wouldn't see me, and I waited.

A few minutes later, Mrs. Crowe headed for the checkout with an armful of books, and I trotted over to the shelf and read a few of the other titles from the shelf she'd been raiding.

A CHRISTIAN WOMAN'S GUIDE TO DIVORCE
HOW TO START A DIVORCE
A NEW LIFE: THE HAPPY DIVORCÉE

The theme was clear. My first thought was to feel sad for Mrs. Crowe, and her soon-to-be-ex-husband. Maybe if they had read my yet-to-be-written book, they could have saved their marriage.

Chapter Nine
GUESSING GAMES

It was not jealousy that drove the Countess Ravishia to set fire to the hair of her seventeenth lover, Guido Barkwallow, but rather an inclination to making separations as memorable and unambiguous as possible.

— from *Wrathlust Hollow* **by Carmelita Woldstonecraft**

LITA

When I walked into the house I heard the soft rattle of my mother's fingers on the computer keyboard. It was a reassuring sound, one I'd been hearing for as long as I could remember. She would be sitting at her desk wearing sweatpants and a funky, old sweater, totally immersed in some imagined romance.

I tried to close the door softly so that I could grab a juice box out of the fridge without bothering her. It didn't work. She can hear like a bat when she wants to.

The typing stopped. "Lydia, is that you?"

"That was me being as quiet as humanly possible," I said. "And I wish you wouldn't call me that."

"It's your name," she said.

I walked over to her office door. "Chosen without my consent." I wondered if we were about to have another fight.

She lowered her glasses and looked at me over the computer screen. Behind her on the wall was an enormous poster of the cover of her four-teenth novel, *Heartless*, featuring a bare-chested Viking named Thorn Broadsword.

"Lydia is a perfectly serviceable name," she said.

"You wouldn't use it for one of your heroines," I said.

"I would, and I have. Lydia Fallsworth. In *Untamable*."

"I mean today — in this century — you wouldn't. You wrote *Untamable* years before I was born."

We'd had this discussion a thousand times already. I don't know why we kept pounding at it. She decided to change the subject.

"Your father called. He'll be in LA for another week. I'm on deadline. We are having Indian takeout for dinner. Please set the table." She lowered her glasses and resumed her typing.

That was my mom when she was in writing mode. Bing, bang, bung. All business even though she was probably in the middle of describing the heaving bosom of a virgin contessa being ravished by a hot-blooded buccaneer with scimitar-cruel lips and eyes like shards of hot ice.

The good news was that she had apparently gotten past the "sticky middle" of her book. In other words, she'd be off my case for a while.

ADAM

I figured that the best way to get something done was to just do it, so as soon as I got home I booted up and started typing.

The first thing you have to know about teenagers is that they are not perfect. However, if you have no expectations of someone, they may appear to be perfect, or nearly so, or if nearly perfect, then higher expectations could possibly contain the possibility of complete perfection, or close enough to suit most perfection-seekers' needs, imperfections aside, in an imperfect world.

Brilliant! I thought.

Then I read it over and it didn't look so good. In fact, it made no sense whatsoever.

Maybe this book-writing thing would be harder than I thought.

DELETE

To save myself from further literary embarrassment, I called Lita to tell her about Mrs. Crowe.

"Lita! Guess what!"

"You're growing a goatee."

"No, I — what?"

"You found out your real father is Thorn Broadsword."

"I — who?"

"Never mind. Look, if you have something to tell me, just tell me. Don't ask me to guess."

"Okay, okay. Jeez, what's *with* you?"

"I'm suffering from teen angst so I'm taking it out on my friends."

"Oh . . . that's okay, then. So, I was at the library downtown and —"

"The library? Oh my God, has hell frozen up again? Why are you *tell-ing* me this? You're giving me brain cramps!"

"You want to hear this or not?"

Lita didn't say anything for almost two seconds — possibly a record.

"Okay," she said at last. "What?"

"I was at the library and guess who — I mean, I saw Mrs. Crowe."

"You saw a *librarian* at a *library*? How odd."

"Guess what — no, wait, she was looking at books about divorce. I think the Crowes are getting divorced."

Once again, Lita went a long time without saying anything. Finally, she cleared her throat and said, "That's kinda sad."

LITA

I felt bad for Mrs. Crowe, even if she was a major priss-butt. Also, I had this nagging feeling that it was *possible* that Miz Fitz's investigation into her trash *maybe* had something to do with it. If so, then Mrs. Crowe was right about my blog being dangerous. On the other hand, she had thrown her husband's Viagra in the trash last year so maybe the breakup had been inevitable.

"What were you doing at the library?" I asked Adam.

"Working on my book."

"Book?" I'd assumed that the book thing was just another of Adam's passing fantasies.

"My book about what guys and girls really want," he said.

Okay, now *that* was so funny my laugh reflex completely froze up. I switched the phone to my other ear and managed to say, "Wait a second — you're *serious*?"

"It's gonna be like a handbook."

"A *hand*book? It would take a book the size of the Library of Congress to even make a dent in that subject."

"I'm having some trouble getting started."

He sounded so pathetic I couldn't help giving him some advice. "My mom says that the best way to start a book is by doing research. Maybe you should check out the books that are already out there."

"That's a good idea. I don't want to reinvent the horse."

"Wheel."

"What?"

"It's reinventing the *wheel*. Not the *horse*."

"Oh. Hey, guess who . . ." He scowled. "Y'know, it's no fun telling you stuff if I can't make you guess!"

"Okay, you can make me guess this one time."

"Guess who I'm sitting right between in calculus."

I knew the answer immediately. "Dennis and the Skank."

"I . . . how do you *do* that?"

"I'm psychic."

"Seriously," he said. "How did you know?"

"Elementary, my dear Merchant. There are a limited number of people who we both know. Dennis would be taking calc, of course. And the only other person in this school you would find it interesting in relation to Dennis other than Emily, who is as likely to sign up for

58

calculus as you are to go out for synchronized swimming, is Blair Thompson. Voilà."

"Can you believe she's taking calculus?"

"I can't believe *you're* taking calculus!"

"I need it to get into a top business college."

"What you *need* are straight As and a pair of rich parents. Neither of which you have."

"So I'll go to a mediocre business college. Unless I make a million bucks on my book."

"Yeah, right."

"I signed up for Ms. Ling's creative writing class. You took that last year, didn't you?"

"Yeah. She's pretty cool," I said.

"Do you think she's really Miz Fitz?"

The rumor about Ms. Ling being Miz Fitz had started last fall, when Ms. Ling, in her first year of teaching, announced her interest in blogging. She created a LiveJournal blog called *23 Voices* and invited all twenty-three students in her creative writing class to blog their hearts out. I quickly learned that many of things I *wanted* to say in my blog were not acceptable — unless I wanted to be ostracized by everyone, including my friends. So I posted boring stuff just like everybody else, but I also started a second blog under the secret identity of Miz Fitz. Then I hacked into the school computer and put links to my blog throughout the Wellstone High website. It took Mr. Birdwell, Wellstone's sorry excuse for an IT expert, three weeks to scour the site, but by that time Miz Fitz was well established, must-reading for the

Wellstone cyber-addict contingent, especially after my notorious garbage survey.

"I doubt it," I said to Adam. "Miz Fitz is way too snarky. Besides, I can't see Ms. Ling digging through Mrs. Crowe's garbage can."

After we hung up I spent a few minutes feeling slightly ill. Something about Adam working on a book of his own really bugged me. What about *my* book? I thought about all the hours I'd spent blogging and texting and talking on the phone while *my* novel sat moldering in its drawer. I hadn't looked at it in months. That is not a good way to finish a novel.

Staring sightlessly at my computer screen, I wallowed in that very special feeling of being worthless and deprived. After a few minutes, I unleashed a deliberately theatrical sigh and opened the bottom desk drawer, dug out a three-ring notebook, opened it, and stared at the title page.

Wrathlust Hollow

I began to read.

Blackness filled Wrathlust Hollow like the sludge in the bottom of a forgotten cup of hot cocoa. Suddenly, an earsplitting scream punctured the viscous night air . . .

After one page I wanted to dope slap myself for printing it out in such an old-fashioned, hard-to-read font, but after a few more pages I got used to it.

The Countess Ravishia, desirous of the attentions of one Guido Barkwallow, sent a messenger bearing a single black rose. Guido, knowing that all of the mad countess's previous lovers had come to bad ends, wept. Still, he was unable to resist her summons, and set forth immediately for Wanderlust.

One hundred seven pages later, with the mad Countess Ravishia hanging by her fingertips to the parapets of Glandish Castle, and the Unaligned Nations of the Western Verge engaged in battle with the armies of Wanderlust, the story ended. Or rather, it stopped. I would have to write another two hundred pages if I wanted to finish it.

I put it back in the drawer.

Finish it? Why would I do that?

It was total crap.

ADAM

Lita was right. If I wanted to write a book, I would have to do some more research. I began online, googling the phrases *what boys want* and *men + women + differences*. I found excerpts from several books, a few semi-interesting newsgroups, and dozens of chat rooms, joke pages, and magazine articles. Every time I ran across something good I copied it and pasted it into a document:

• Men are designed to focus on a single task: Kill the antelope and drag it home. Women are programmed to protect and nurture several children at once — they can't afford to focus on just one thing.

• When a man walks into a room he looks for danger and escape routes. Women look at the other people's faces to find out how they feel.

• Girls mature faster than boys. Sixteen-year-old boys are still playing video games and giving each other wedgies after gym class. This is the reason few high school romances last.

I copied about fifty little snippets like that. At first, I was so excited to find all that great stuff that I thought that I could just put a bunch of it together and I'd have a book. But there were two problems with that.

First, most of it wasn't all that *useful*, and I wanted my book to be chock-full of practical advice. Like what do you do when a girl asks you out, and you like her, but her brother is a psycho-moron who hates you? And what should a girl say when a boy compliments her on the size of her breasts? And how do you handle it when the boy likes the Monkey Fart Shriekers, and the girl is into Taylor Swift?

Second, I wasn't sure whether it was okay for me to just copy stuff off the web and put it in a book. I would have to rewrite the stuff I liked, and try to make it sound more useful. I started with a paragraph copied from some university website:

When groups of boys and groups of girls are trying to find their way out of a maze, the boys usually establish a leader, and explore the maze by sending out scouts while remaining within hearing distance of each other. Girls stay together and wander in a group until they find their way out.

How could I make that into something a real person could actually use? I thought for a moment, then dove in, cutting, pasting, and adding words until I had something that looked completely different:

When groups of boys and groups of girls are trying to find their way out of a maze, the boys pick a leader. The leader is usually the boy who has the best luck with girls, because girls like guys with power. Then the boys send out scouts while remaining within hearing distance of each other. Girls stay together and wander in a herd, all talking at the same time, until they find their way out. The thing to know is that boys are better at solving problems once they decide who's in charge, while girls just walk and talk until the problem goes away.

I reread what I had written. *Pretty good,* I thought.
I kept at it.

Chapter Ten
BIOLOGY

Dear Miz Fitz,

Why do girls fall in love so easily?

— Fallen Angel

Miz Fitz sez:

EASILY? I suppose you think it's EASY to get hit by a bus. There is nothing EASY about it!

LITA

I got to school twenty minutes early and went straight to the library to get a look at Mrs. Crowe. I don't know why I expected her to look any different. But I had to see.

Mrs. Crowe was nowhere in sight, but Miss Morris was sitting behind the desk checking in books that had been dropped through the slot after hours.

"Hi, Miss M," I said.

She looked up scowling and blinking, then she smiled.

"Lita, you're up early today!"

"I thought I'd get a head start on biology class. Do you have any books about slime molds or frog dissection?"

Miss Morris chuckled and went back to scanning her pile of returns. That was one of the things that made her so cool. You could never put one over on her, but she didn't mind you trying. If I'd said the same thing to Mrs. Crowe, she would have had me in the slime mold and frog section in a second.

"So . . . where's Mrs. C?" I asked, all casual and innocent-like.

Miss Morris gave me that cocked eyebrow look that means, *I know you're up to something, young lady.* But instead of confronting me, she said, "Mrs. Crowe won't be in for a week or two."

"Oh," I said. "Why?"

Miss Morris crossed her arms and sat back. "Is there something I can help you with, Lita?"

"No," I said. "I mean, yes. Is she getting divorced?"

Miss Morris took her time replying. After about six-and-a-half *really uncomfortable* seconds, she said, "Setting aside — for the moment — the fact that Mrs. Crowe's personal life is none of your business, why would you ask me something like that?"

"Overwhelming curiosity?"

"Lita . . ." she sighed. "I suppose a lecture about boundaries would sail right past you. . . ."

"Probably," I agreed.

"All right, since it might keep you from further prying, I'll tell you that Mrs. Crowe is visiting her sister in Nevada, who has taken ill. Mrs. Crowe has taken a leave of absence to stay with her sister during her recovery."

"Oh."

"What made you think she was getting divorced?"

"Somebody told me."

"Who —" Her lips clamped together, and she made a dismissive wave with both hands. "Never mind, I don't want to know. I *really* do not want to know." She pointed to the far corner of the library. "You will find your slime molds in the nature section."

I backed off, knowing that I had pushed Miss Morris to the brink. I went to the magazine section and started flipping through the latest issue of *Elle*, wondering if "visiting her sister in Nevada" was a coded way of spelling out D-I-V-O-R-C-E.

ADAM

I woke up on the bus.

That's what it felt like, anyway. I hazily recalled my mom spritzing me awake with her plant mister. Next thing I knew I was dragging on a pair of jeans, shoving a piece of toast in my mouth, then staggering toward the bus stop.

"You okay?"

I looked at Bob Glaus, who was sitting next to me.

"I didn't get much sleep last night," I said.

"How come?"

"Working on my book." I yawned one of those shuddering, jaw-dislocating yawns.

"*Dude,*" said Bob, leaning away from me. "Forget to brush your teeth this morning?"

I tasted the inside of my mouth. It wasn't *that* bad.

"You got a mint or something?" I asked.

The kid sitting in front of us turned around, holding out a tin of Altoids.

"Take two," he said.

LITA

I ran into Adam on the way to my first-hour class. He looked particularly scruffy. I sidled up beside him and said, "Adam. You look like crap. And by *crap*, I mean *shit*."

"Thanks," he said. "You look lovely as well."

"How's the book coming along?" I asked, even though I kind of didn't want to know.

"Great!" He grinned his Adam grin, which canceled out most of the scruffiness. "I wrote seventeen pages last night!"

"You did?" I have to admit I was astounded.

"I was up till four this morning!"

"You have the boy-girl thing all figured out?" I said. Adam, of course, didn't notice the layers of irony in my voice.

"I'm getting there." He stopped in front of Mr. Hallgren's classroom. "I'm here," he said. "Where do you go?"

"Biology."

"Prepping for the inevitable rat dissection?"

"Frogs, I believe."

"Later, Leeter."

I headed for biology thinking, *Seventeen pages!* Adam could be scary productive when he set his mind to it, like the time he helped me win the swim-team fund-raiser contest by selling twenty-six buckets of cookie dough door-to-door in one afternoon. But I still had trouble with the concept of him writing an entire book. Adam was not a literary kind of guy. I once tried to get him to read *Pride and Prejudice*. He never made it past the part where Mr. Bennett refuses to call on Mr. Bingley, and that was on page two!

I found Emily, my lab partner, sitting at the back of the room, looking morose. She had traded in her heels for a pair of green high-tops. The rest of her was covered with camouflage capris and an oversize T-shirt decorated with dark green parrots.

I sat down beside her.

"Hey, partner," I said. "Planning to ambush a wildebeest?"

"Maybe," she said, not looking at me. Her eyes were fixed on Dennis, who was sitting at the front of the room laughing about something — probably mildew or flatworms — with fellow science nerd Gene Rudman.

"Y'know, you aren't much fun when you're in lust," I said.

"I know."

"Did you know Adam is writing a book?" I asked, hoping to drag her out of her funk.

"I ordered a copy yesterday," she said. "It's called *What Boys and Girls Want*."

I laughed out loud. Emily scowled.

"That is so Adam!" I said. "Selling a book he hasn't even written yet."

"It was only ten dollars. He gave me a money-back guarantee."

I stared at her, realizing for the first time the depths of her desperation. I reached out and put my hand on her arm.

"Emily, if you really want Dennis . . ."

"I do!"

"Then I'll help you get him."

Chapter Eleven
SALES TECHNIQUES

Dear Miz Fitz,

Why do boys eat so fast?

— Sendmeurlove

Miz Fitz sez:

Because they lack conversational skills. Next time you are on a dinner date with a boy, pay attention to how much you talk compared to how much he talks. Chances are, you'll get in six words to his one. And what is he doing while you are talking? Shoveling.

ADAM

"C'mon," I said. "Everything you ever wanted to know about girls for a lousy ten bucks."

"What if I don't want to know anything?" Robbie asked, adding a layer of potato chips to his hamburger. Wellstone High cafeteria burgers need all the help they could get. "I got enough reading to do. My

70

parents hired me a tutor for English. He's making me read, like, a book a week."

"You don't have to *read* my book," I said. "Just *buy* it."

"Why should we buy a book you haven't even written?" said Bob.

"I need the money to get it printed," I said. "That's why I'm offering this special discounted price to my best friends."

Dennis, who was pretending to read his biology text while he ogled Blair Thompson, said, "What makes you think you know anything about girls? I don't see you beating them away with a stick."

"It's a science," I said, knowing the way to Dennis's heart. "A matter of observation and deduction."

"It's not science, it's voodoo," said Stuey. Stuey Herrell held the distinction of being the tallest kid in school. The basketball coach had been stalking him for two years, but Stuey preferred to spend his spare hours drinking beer and working on his chronically disabled Toyota pickup truck.

"It's not voodoo *or* science," said Bob. "It's an art."

"Whatever it is, I'm not gonna buy a book about it," Stuey said. "I do just fine with the ladies."

That cracked us all up.

"Since when do *you* do *anything* with the ladies?" Bob said.

"They find me adorable," Stuey said with a straight face.

I stood up and walked over to one of the tables occupied exclusively by the opposite sex. Not the Beautiful Girls' Table or the Cheerleaders' Table or the Scary Girls' table. It was one of the Regular Girls' tables.

"Good afternoon, ladies," I said.

Erica Smith said, "Hi, Adam. Do you need to copy somebody's homework?"

"No! I just wanted to ask you all a question. A survey, like."

"Go ahead," said Gennifer Johanson. Gennifer used to be the most beautiful girl in the eighth grade, but that was before she discovered the joys of overeating.

"What do you think I'm thinking right now?" I asked.

The answers came in a rush.

"You want to borrow money."

"You're thinking about cars."

"You're thinking about sex."

"He's thinking about what we're gonna say we think he's thinking about."

That last one — a pretty good guess — came from the ultra-petite Sarah Rosen, who was marginally cute in a pointy sort of way. I'd always thought that she and Dennis would make a good match — except for the minor glitch that Sarah hated all boys on principle.

I said, "I was thinking that if boys knew what girls were thinking, and girls knew what boys were thinking, then we could all communicate on a more mature level."

They all gaped at me for a couple of seconds, then Erica said, "I don't think I want you to *know* what I'm thinking."

"But you want to know what boys are thinking, right?"

"Well, sure, but . . . get real."

I sat down between Erica and Gennifer and went into my pitch.

I took three orders. Even Sarah Rosen promised to buy a copy later.

Since I was on a roll, I looked around for other potential customers. Wellstone High has three lunch periods, with about five hundred students in each. Each long table seats twelve kids, give or take, and there are forty-eight tables, so some tables are packed, and some have only a few residents — mostly outcasts or kids with body-odor problems. Seniors — the few who don't take advantage of their off-campus privileges — take the tables farthest away from the food line. Freshmen and sophomores sit at the front of the room. I looked over the middle section, where I'd find most of the kids I knew. My eye kept going back to the table where Blair Thompson was sitting with Dahlia Delaney and Chelsea Whalenburg.

I looked back at Dennis, who was still pretending to read his biology book. *Might as well give it a shot,* I thought. I walked over and sat down next to Blair Thompson, who I'd never actually spoken to before, and said, "Aren't you in Mr. Sklansky's calc class?"

Blair gave me a heavy-lidded look, the one that says, *Puh-leeze, you are boring me comatose in front of my friends!*

Chelsea said, "Hi, Adam." Chelsea was one of only eight or nine black students in the school — Wellstone High is not exactly what you'd call multicultural. I didn't know her very well, but we'd had a few classes together, and she seemed nice. Her hair was braided in a way that must have taken hours. You have to admire that kind of dedication.

"Hi," I said, nodding to her and Dahlia, a tiny girl with enormous eyes and multicolored hair. Dahlia liked to wear oversize men's shirts and baggy jeans that dragged on the ground, making her look about ten years old. She stared back at me wordlessly.

The table had the feel of three girls who were sitting together not by choice, but by process of elimination.

Directing myself to Chelsea — the only one who had demonstrated an ability to speak — I said, "Do you know what I'm thinking right now?"

None of them replied at first, then Blair said, "How do we know you're thinking at all? Maybe you're just experiencing a random firing of synapses. Like you're in a vegetative state. Vegetating."

"Wrong," I said, wondering what "random firing of synapses" meant.

I launched into my pitch. Dahlia seemed to be listening, but I had the feeling that she wasn't hearing my words. She was listening the way you would listen to distant music, picking up on the beat. Blair maintained her why-are-you-boring-me look. Chelsea seemed the most receptive of the three, but when it came time to ask them to cough up ten bucks, she just laughed.

"Ten *dollars*? I already *know* what *boys* want, and it's always the same thing. You want me to pay *ten dollars* to read *that*? I can go home and look at my own ass in the *mirror. That's* what *boys* want!"

Dahlia broke up laughing.

Blair asked, "Will your book explain how come your friend with the open mouth keeps staring at me?" She pointed with her fork at Dennis, who immediately ducked his head behind his biology text.

"Absolutely," I said.

"Girl," said Chelsea, "you *know* why he's *staring* at you."

Dahlia dissolved into a puddle of high-pitched giggles and gasps.

Chelsea said, "What about boners? Will it explain boners?"

"Boners?" I felt my face getting hot.

"Yeah," said Chelsea. "Like, how often do you get them."

"Like, do you have one right now?" asked Blair.

"No!" I didn't, but I was afraid to stand up because when I did, they'd all be looking at my crotch.

This marketing thing was turning out to be more complicated than I'd thought.

Chapter Twelve
SCHEMING
(PART ONE)

Miz Fitz,

I am one of those Y-chromosome types you like to rag on, but I have a serious question. Why don't girls just say what they mean instead of beating around the bush?

— Frustrated Male

Miz Fitz sez:

Have you not been listening?

LITA

I was sitting in my favorite seat in the back corner of the library staring at the question I had written in my notebook.

How do you convince a guy to fall in love with a girl he thinks is wallpaper, especially when the guy is obsessed with someone else?

I kept going over and over the situation in my mind. I had told Emily I would help her, but *how*?

The problem demanded a two-pronged approach.

Prong One: Drive a wedge between Dennis and Blair. That was, you might say, my specialty. I had been sabotaging Adam's love life for years — in his own interest, of course.

Prong Two: Make Dennis look at Emily the way he looked at Blair.

I decided to concentrate on Prong One. I could deal with making Emily irresistible later.

There are many ways for a girl to turn a guy off. I made a list:

Emit unpleasant odors
Talk too loud
Talk with mouth full of food
Scratch private areas in public

I stopped writing and fought back a twinge of queasiness. Short of dosing her with laxatives, itching powder, garlic extract, and other noxious substances, I didn't see how I could get Blair to make herself repulsive in those ways.

Reading through the list again, I realized that what I had just described was a boy. Did that mean that boys were secretly repelled by themselves? Or were belching, farting, stinking, scratching, and spitting repellent only when practiced by females? (I have to admit, a girl scratching her crotch grosses me out more than a boy doing it. When I see a boy doing it I figure he needs a shower. When I see a girl with her hand down there, I think cooties.)

I continued with the list of repellent behaviors.

> Laugh at him in front of his friends
> Report him to the police for stalking
> Make him feel stupid.

Hmm . . . maybe I was onto something. How far would Emily want me to go? If she was desperate enough to drop $120 on a pair of über-skank high heels — not to mention wearing them to school — she might approve of anything short of kidnapping.

For a moment — *only* for a moment — I wished I still had my doll collection.

When I was a little girl I named my dolls after people I knew. I had dolls for all my friends at school, and for my parents and the neighbors, and for all kinds of made-up people. I would spend hours sending them on dates, making them marry, fight, have babies, break up, go for wild rides down the banister — occasionally resulting in a loss of limbs or heads — get back together, have sex (I later learned that I had the sex part all wrong — it has nothing to do with inserting breasts into armpits), and die. If I had my dolls now, I could run Dennis and Emily and Blair and me and Adam and everybody else I knew through all the dating combinations. It would be fun.

But very, very immature. In any case, when I was thirteen I gave my entire doll collection to my cousin Allie for her fourth birthday. It had seemed like a very grown-up thing to do, but there were times I still regretted it.

Pulling myself back to reality, I once again scanned my list.

I thought hard for a few seconds, then wrote a few lines in my notebook.

It was underhanded. It was sneaky. It was dishonest.

It was foolproof.

Emily would be so pleased.

Chapter Thirteen
TERRITORIAL DISPUTE

Dear Miz Fitz,
I have a stalker. How do you turn a guy off?
— *Maid Marian*

Miz Fitz sez:

This can be accomplished by using strong odors (intestinal gases), unpleasant noises (speaking endlessly on topics such as chastity and early marriage), visual assault (get you ugly), or tactile stimulation (scratching, kicking, biting, etc.) In severe cases, it may be necessary to apply several such techniques simultaneously.

ADAM

Fifth period — what ought to be siesta time — I was having trouble paying attention to Mr. Sklansky's "quick review" of quadratic equations. But it wasn't because I was sleepy. It was because I had sixty dollars in my pocket, plus several people who'd promised to bring in money later that week, and all I could think about was how much money

I was going to make on the book — and what the hell was I going to write about boners?

During lunch, I had talked to twenty-two girls and five boys, and had taken eleven orders. That was a forty percent success rate!

The bad news was that the boys didn't buy any books. Guys didn't seem to want to know what girls really wanted.

It was a bad news–good news situation. My potential customer base was only fifty percent of the population — that was the bad news. The good news? I only had to write about what *boys* wanted to get the girls to buy it. I figured I could wrap that up in less than a hundred pages.

I ran through the numbers. Not the numbers Mr. Sklansky was chalking onto the board, but the numbers in my head. Sixteen hundred students at Wellstone. Half were girls. If half of the eight hundred girls bought a copy of the book, that would be four hundred books at ten bucks each, or $4,000. And that was just this one school! I could also hit the middle school, and the other high schools in the area, and . . . I could sell millions! I could —

"Ow!" Something jabbed my left shoulder. I looked at Blair, who had used the sharp point of her pencil to get my attention. She jerked her head toward the front of the room where Mr. Sklansky was standing, arms crossed, eyes drilling into me.

"Welcome back, Mr. Merchant," he said. "Did you have a nice nap?"

Several students snickered, including both Dennis and Blair.

I said, "Sorry. I was running some numbers in my head."

"I'm sure you were." He pointed at an equation on the board. "Was it any of these numbers, perchance?"

"Not exactly."

"I thought as much." Mr. Sklansky's voice was dry as chalk. He sighed and turned back to the board, muttering something about martyrs and early retirement.

After class, Dennis chased me down in the hall.

"That was amazing," he said. "Sklansky called on you, like, five times and you were just *gone*. And then Blair poked you — she is so cool."

"Since when does poking me make somebody cool?"

"It was the way she did it."

A new voice came from behind us. "Nice one back there."

We stopped and turned. It was Blair, giving me her heavy-lidded look.

I didn't know what to say, because I couldn't tell whether she meant "Nice one back there!" as in "Cool! You really messed with Sklansky's head," or as in "You are such a pathetic moron," or as in "Nice boner!"

So I said, "Uh . . ." But at least this time I didn't blush.

Blair shifted her mascaraed gaze to Dennis, who looked as if he was about to faint. "I hope you plan to help him with his calculus, Dennis." She smiled, her dark red lipstick making her teeth look unnaturally bright. "He's going to need it."

She walked away, leaving both Dennis and me openmouthed.

"What was *that* about?" I asked.

Dennis said, "She knows my name!"

"Well, good for you. She thinks *I'm* a moron." I don't know why I cared, but I did.

Dennis said, "She's magnificent."

LITA

I zombied my way through my last class thinking about my plan for de-infatuating Dennis from Blair. The more I thought about my idea, the crazier it seemed. Crazy but effective. Best not to tell Emily a thing; that way she would have deniability later on. I wasn't even sure I was up to it. I kept flip-flopping, first thinking what a great idea I'd had and getting all excited, then I'd kind of crash and wonder if I was really helping Emily or about to perform an evil act out of sheer depravity. Outside of being skanky and weird, Blair Thompson had never done anything to me and neither had Dennis. On the other hand, I might be doing them both a favor.

After the last bell, I shoved my dilemma aside and headed for home. I ran into Adam on the steps outside the school.

"If it isn't the Future Famous Author," I said. Before, it had been just sort of funny — I guess I hadn't really believed that he was going to *do* it — but it was starting to get under my skin.

"Do you even have a title yet?" I asked.

"I was going to call it *The Battle of the Sexes*. But the book isn't really about the battle, it's more about what guys and girls *want*. So then I decided to call it *What Boys and Girls Want*. Except when I started selling it this morning, I found out that boys don't buy books."

"That's because most of them can't read."

"They read, but mostly just sports or sci-fi or joke books. So I'm calling my book *What Boys Want*, and then selling it mostly to girls. What do you think?"

I had to admit, the title was catchy.

"I'm going to publish it myself," he said. "Hey, there's Tracy. I bet she'll order a copy. . . ."

And he was gone, leaving me feeling sour and neglected and suddenly pissed off at the world. I started for home, trying to sort out my feelings. I got that Adam was this hyperactive entrepreneur type who was going to do all sorts of things in his life, but why did he have to write a *book*?

I'm supposed to be the writer. He *knows* that. Ever since we were kids he's known that I want to write novels, so why was he trespassing on my territory?

On a conscious level, I realized I was being illogical and jealous, and if I wanted to be a writer I should just sit down and finish my stupid book and not get all twisted just because somebody else wanted to do the same thing. Still, it ate at me. You know how it is when you get really mad about something but you know if you say anything you'll look like a petty, insecure fool? You know how you just want to *explode*?

So I exploded, a big *ka-thunk* deep inside my chest. It almost felt good. The funny thing was, the explosion didn't go in the direction of Adam and his stupid book.

It went toward Blair.

Chapter Fourteen
SEX AFTER FIFTY AND OTHER APPALLING ACTS

It was not enough for the Countess Ravishia to have besotted every eligible man in Wrathlust. She also put considerable effort into undermining the romantic hopes of the other noblewomen. As, for example, when she had Lady Horcroft's secret lover beheaded for failing to doff his cap.

— **from** *Wrathlust Hollow* **by Carmelita Woldstonecraft**

ADAM

How long does it take to write a book?

I figured if I wrote ten pages a day, I could finish in a couple weeks. But that night I stalled out at three pages. I'd used up all the obvious, easy-to-find stuff on the web, and I kept getting stuck trying to organize the book. Like, should I do short chapters, or long sections, or break it up by topic, or what?

I needed a model, so I ran downstairs and went through the bookshelves in the living room. Nothing but novels and history books. No self-help.

I found my dad on the screen porch working a sudoku and smoking one of his pipes.

"You know you're committing slow-motion suicide, don't you?" I said. I'd been bugging him about his pipe smoking for years with little effect.

"How's it going, kiddo?" he asked with a smoky grin.

"Do we have any of those books around? You know, about how to become a better person and stuff."

He set down his puzzle and peered at me over the tops of his reading glasses. "Could you be more specific?"

"Like Mom reads. Like that one she was reading about understanding teenagers? Or the ones about living fearlessly and discovering the power within?"

"Self-help books?"

"Yeah. I can't find any."

"Check the basement," he said. "Your mother recently thinned out the bookshelves. I think she plans to donate all her self-help books to the church rummage sale. She read a self-help book that told her self-help books were worthless." My father has a very dry sense of humor. "What do you need help with?" he asked.

"I'm looking for guidance," I said. "I think I might skip college."

It's hard to describe what happened to his face just then, but it must have hurt.

"Just kidding!" I said quickly.

He closed his eyes, put his hand over his heart, and took a deep breath. "Adam, don't *do* that!"

"It's for a school project." Giving him an all-purpose answer that would not require explanation.

"I see. Well. Good luck with that."

I found the book box under the stairs and sorted through it. I had hit a self-help gold mine. Titles included *Understanding Your Teenager*, *The Power Within*, *Finding God in Everyday Life*, *Sex After Fifty* — just the title of that one practically made me hurl — and *Meditations for Parents Who Do Too Much*. I paged through them. The problem was, they were all different. Some of them were full of quotes from famous people, and the author would riff on the quote. Some were like instruction manuals, some were more like exercise books, and as for *Sex After Fifty* — believe me, you do *not* want to know. The one that interested me most was a slim hardcover book called *Questions for Elton*.

Questions for Elton was a bunch of questions that the author, a nerdy-looking guy named Noah Silverman, asked this old coal miner named Elton Gumm, who was dying from black lung. I thought most of the questions were pretty stupid — stuff like "Are you afraid of dying?"

The correct answer, of course, is "Well, *duh!*" But Elton Gumm manages to go on for five or six pages on the topic. So it was a really dumb book overall, but I liked the question-answer format.

It looked totally poachable.

LITA

Chelsea Whalenburg was outspoken to a fault, afraid of no one, and friendly with Blair, which made her the perfect tool for my nefarious purposes. My only problem was that I didn't really know her. And she scared me a little.

It was two days before I found my chance to get Chelsea alone. I spotted her after school, after the buses had left, leaning against an aging SUV in the student parking lot with her arms crossed and a tight frown on her face. She looked about as approachable as a pissed-off water buffalo. I took a deep breath and headed toward her. Her eyes flicked at me, then went back to staring at the school building. I was no part of her current reality.

I walked as if I was heading for the other end of the parking lot, but when I passed by Chelsea I stopped, as if paralyzed by a sudden thought.

"Hi, Chelsea," I said.

She looked over at me, surprised.

"Hey," she said. She didn't even know my name.

"Waiting for somebody?" I asked.

She didn't say anything, giving me the look of suspicion and distrust I deserved.

After a few seconds she said, "I'm waiting on that fool Andrew James. He's supposed to give me a ride home, only he's not here." She kicked the fender of the SUV with her heel. "I guess I should've taken the bus." She went back to staring at the school with an intensity that almost made me believe she could see through brick. "I'm gonna have that boy's balls."

Did I say she scared me a little? I lied. She scared me a lot. Chelsea had a reputation for saying whatever was on her mind, which was a little scary, but the main reason she scared me was because she was black. I wasn't scared of her blackness exactly, it was more like I was scared I'd say something stupid, or look at her wrong, and she would despise me for being a suburban white-bread ignoramus, which was pretty much true.

"You got a car?" she asked, sliding her eyes in my direction.

"Sorry," I said.

She looked away, losing all interest in me.

I decided to take the plunge. I said, "Pretty weird about Dennis and Blair, huh?"

Her forehead wrinkled. I gave her a few seconds to catch up.

"Dennis who?" she asked.

"Dennis Long? Always staring at Blair?

"Oh. Him." She retained her puzzled look, waiting for more.

I let her wait.

"What about them?" she finally asked.

I shrugged like it was really nothing, then said, "I guess they're going out or something. The odd couple."

Chelsea laughed and went back to staring through the brick walls of the school. After about three seconds she looked back at me. "Seriously?"

"That's what Dennis says. He says she's hot for him. She's been calling him."

"Blair? Calling him?"

"Uh-huh."

"I don't *think* so."

"Well, that's what he says. I guess she's really into him."

Chelsea gave me a you-must-be-out-of-your-mind look. I decided to slather on another layer of unlikelihood.

"So, does Blair really have a birthmark shaped like a bunny rabbit on her butt?"

Chelsea shook her head, not quite believing she was having this conversation. "I'm in her gym class, and I never saw no *bunny* on her ass. Not that I was looking. Who told you she had a bunny on her ass?"

"I'm pretty sure it was Dennis," I said.

It's not as if I didn't know I'd done something heinous and vile. I knew. But in the larger scheme of things (my best friend's happiness being of overriding importance), I felt that my actions were defensible. Anyway, that would be my justification.

But it took me quite a while to get the nerve up to call Emily. In the end, I decided to spare her the details of what I had done.

"I am giving you the gift of deniability," I said when she answered the phone.

"Oh, good," she said, "I was hoping for diamonds, but deniability, well, what girl doesn't want deniability?"

"Believe me, you might need it," I said. "I have performed a service for you. The Blair problem has been dealt with. Dennis is yours for the taking. Or he will be, once the shit hits the fan."

"What shit?" she asked. "What fan?"

Chapter Fifteen
THE BIG YELLOW DOG

Dear Miz Fitz,
When do you just say the hell with it, and give up?
— Unrequited

Miz Fitz sez:
Not until he gets a restraining order.

LITA

The next morning I left the house feeling what my mother would have called "out of sorts." Which makes no sense at all. What "sorts" was I supposed to be out of? I was thinking about this and other nonsensical things the semi-famous Amanda Maize liked to say, getting mad at her even though we hadn't exchanged a word that morning (she was already in her office typing when I got up) and, at the same time, trying to figure out why I was all bent about something she hadn't even said. At least not lately. It doesn't take much for me to get mad at my mother.

By the time I got to school, I'd decided that it wasn't my mom I was really mad at. It was Emily, who had stupidly fallen for Dennis, who was besotted with Blair, and somehow it had fallen on me to fix things for her, forcing me to tell Chelsea that ridiculous story and possibly screwing up my karma for the next six lifetimes. I'd probably be reborn as a dung beetle.

ADAM

I caught up with Lita in the school foyer, a swarm of sleepy students milling about us on all sides.

"Hey, Lita, what are the main things girls want to know about guys?"

Lita gave me a look that made me take a step back. Uh-oh. She was in one of her moods.

"Is this for your *book*?" she said.

"Uh . . . yeah."

"Here's one," she said. "Why are boys so self-centered and unaware?"

I wrote that down on the back of my notebook. "What else?" I asked.

"Why do boys think they're the center of the entire universe?"

"Isn't that kind of the same thing?"

She shook her head and started walking; I fell in beside her. "Are you mad at me?"

"Why would I be mad at you?"

She was *definitely* mad at me.

"I don't know," I said. "That's why I asked."

Lita rolled her eyes so hard I could almost hear it. "I just think this book thing has gone to your head. I mean, my mom has written, like, sixty books and she doesn't go around talking about them all the time. And what do you know about boys and girls, anyway? You've got all the awareness of an earthworm."

I'd known Lita long enough to realize that when she got that way the best thing to do was roll over on my back and wag my tail.

"Sorry," I said. "What do you think I should do?" I asked.

Lita stopped and glared at me, trying to find something wrong with my question. I braced myself for another attack, but suddenly, she grinned.

"You could try reading Miz Fitz," she said.

Bestselling authors are not created overnight, so I was glad I'd taken creative writing. I had signed up for it thinking it would be an easy A — but it turned out to be way harder than I'd thought. Ms. Ling wasted no time making us be creative.

"Pens and paper out, please," she said in her soft voice. You would think that to teach a class full of teens you would need a big voice, but Ms. Ling's tiny whisper worked amazingly well. If the classroom wasn't dead quiet, nobody could hear her, so it made us all extra careful not to shuffle our feet or crinkle papers.

"Today, we will write a sentence describing an action: '*A big yellow dog ran into the street.*' I would like ten variations on that sentence from each of you, in ten minutes time." She set the timer on her desk. "Please begin."

I began:

1. THE YELLOW DOG RUNNING ON THE STREET WAS BIG.

2. AN ENORMOUS COWARDLY CANINE PROPELLED ITSELF ACROSS THE ROAD.

3. A DOG THE COLOR OF CORN AND THE SIZE OF A HORSE MOVED SWIFTLY FROM ONE SIDE OF THE ROAD TO THE OTHER.

The first few were easy, but after that things got tough. By the time I reached number seven, I was getting weird:

7. A JAYWALKING SAINT BERNARD THE COLOR OF A PERFECTLY RIPENED BANANA WAS NEARLY HIT BY THE VOLKSWAGEN BEETLE.

That was as far as I got before the timer went off. Ms. Ling made us circle our favorite sentence, then asked how many of us had circled the first sentence we had written.

Nobody raised their hand.

"How many of you circled the second sentence?"

No hands.

One person had circled their third sentence, three had circled the fourth, and so on.

"How many of you liked the *last* sentence you wrote best?"

About two-thirds of us raised our hands.

"Very good," said Ms. Ling.

I left class feeling defeated. What Ms. Ling had just taught us — at least the message I got — was that to write a good sentence, you had to do it over and over and over again. How was I going to finish writing a whole book if I had to do that?

LITA

I would never tell Adam but I spent most of the morning (when I was supposed to be doing other things) thinking about what girls want to know about boys. I came up with nineteen questions including such gems as "What does a wedgie feel like if you have testicles?" Eventually, I whittled it down to ten questions that he might find useful, because even though I was pissed about him writing a book (instead of me writing a book), I felt bad about snapping at him that morning. Besides, nobody likes to see their friends fall flat on their faces.

The other thing I did that morning was think about the bomb I'd planted with Chelsea Whalenburg. How long would it take her to pass it on to Blair? How would Blair react?

I was on the way to the library when I saw Adam and Dennis talking to Blair Thompson. I stopped and watched. They were standing outside one of the math classrooms. Adam was talking (no surprise there), and Blair was laughing and winding a shank of her long, skanky hair around her forefinger while Dennis gawked at her like a love-struck puppy.

Apparently, the Chelsea bomb had yet to detonate.

ADAM

It was easy to see why Dennis had such a tough time with girls. In the first place, he didn't get the concept of small talk. Here I was trying to get him into a conversation with Blair, and every time he opened his mouth, all that came out was a bunch of stuff about calculus, or something he was doing in chemistry, or — worse yet — his *stamp* collection.

Blair was cool, though. She seemed much friendlier than she had when I tried to talk to her at lunch. She smiled and nodded when Dennis spoke, but a second later she would be looking at me — not Dennis.

"How's your book going?" she asked.

"Still working on it." Trying to get Dennis back into the conversation, I said, "Dennis here won't order one."

Dennis said, "I'm saving my money for a new gaming system."

Like I said, pathetic.

Blair said to me, "PlayStation or Xbox?"

"Both," Dennis said.

"I used to play Sims," Blair said with a laugh.

I thought Dennis was about to hug her. "Really? I —"

Fortunately, the bell rang before things got too weird. As we filed into class, Blair made a fist and gave me the lightest possible shoulder punch. "See you in class," she said.

Dennis didn't notice. He was in nirvana. He had actually had a conversation with Blair Thompson. Never mind that he totally botched it. As Sklansky droned on about the difference between differential and integral calculus, Dennis had this dreamy, happy expression on his face. But when I looked at Blair, I caught her looking at me.

LITA

"Hey, Leeter."

"I am not a metric unit," I said without turning my head. I continued reading, which is what you're *supposed* to do in the library.

Adam leaned on the back of my chair. "Then what kind of unit are you?"

I turned around and gave him my best glare. "So now you're hanging out with Blair Thompson? Whatever happened to good taste? Oh, wait, I forgot. You never had any."

"What — I can't talk to Blair?"

"You can talk to anybody you want to." I went back to reading. He came around the other side of the table and sat down across from me.

"I was just trying to get her and Dennis talking," he said.

I gaped at him. "Are you completely brain dead?"

"I don't think so. Why?"

"Why? Because Dennis is for Emily, that's why."

He looked surprised for a second, then he started laughing. At me!

Chapter Sixteen
THE TOP TEN

Dear Miz Fitz,

There is a guy at school I made out with this one time, but that was all we did. Now he's telling everybody I'm a ho. The problem is, everybody believes him.

— Stung

Miz Fitz sez:

You could let him know how hurt you are by his lies. Unless he is actually telling the truth. Ho.

ADAM

I was running out of ideas, and had written only twenty-nine pages. I'd been counting on Lita to help me out, but she was all whacked over the Emily/Dennis/Blair thing. I probably shouldn't have laughed at her. I wasn't too worried, though — Lita had been mad at me so many times I'd lost count, and we had always stayed friends — even after the time she forced her precious copy of *Jane Eyre* on me and insisted I read it, and not only did I not read it, but I left it out in the rain. Lita was always touchy about her books.

I remembered then that Lita had suggested reading Miz Fitz's blog. I knew about the blog, of course — everybody at Wellstone had heard of it after Miz Fitz had gone digging in Mrs. Crowe's garbage last year — but the one time I'd checked it out all I saw was a bunch of advice for girls. Nothing I was interested in — at the time. But maybe Lita was right. Maybe it was just what I needed for my book.

I struck gold immediately. Right there on the first page was Miz Fitz's Top Ten Things Girls Want to Know about Guys.

1. Is it true that boys think about sex every seven seconds?
2. Why do boys think bad smells are funny?
3. Why are boys obsessed with boobs?
4. Why do boys act so immature when they are with other boys?
5. What do boys say when they talk about girls?
6. Why do boys punch each other?
7. Don't they know they look stupid when their mouths hang open?
8. Does he like me?
9. Is he a good kisser?
10. Has he gone all the way?

I tried to imagine Ms. Ling writing that list. No way. I'd never really believed the rumor about her being Miz Fitz. It had to be a student — probably one of the seniors. It could even be Lita — it had that same edgy tone she gets sometimes — except there was no way she wouldn't have told me about it. Lita and I did not keep secrets from each other. Not big, important ones, at least.

I copied the list, then began to answer the questions. I figured I could stretch it out to ten pages. I was on number two — *Why do boys think bad smells are funny?* — when my cell rang.

It was Dennis. "You aren't going to believe this," he said.

"Try me."

"I was walking out of school, and Blair and her friend Chelsea were standing there, and they were, like, looking at me. So I kind of went over to them, and Blair all of a sudden *hit* me for no reason."

"You mean she punched you on the shoulder?" I said, thinking of the gentle, friendly, "see ya later" shoulder punch Blair had laid on me earlier.

Dennis said, "No! She hit me in the *face*."

"A serious hit?"

"A serious *slap*."

"Why?"

"I have no idea. And then you know what she said? This is even weirder."

"What?"

"She said, 'Rabbit on my ass? My *ass*!' And then Chelsea started laughing and I got the hell out of there."

I thought about the three of us standing outside of calc — it was only a couple of hours ago — me talking, Blair laughing, and Dennis with his puppy-dog eyes. Blair hadn't seemed bothered. In fact, the two of them had had a short conversation about video games. Why would she slap him?

"You do ogle her a bit," I said. "Maybe she got tired of being ogled."

"She didn't have to *hit* me. Besides, what was all that about a rabbit?"

"That's a little weird."

"That's a *lot* weird."

"Do you still like her?"

Dennis didn't speak for a few seconds, then, "I don't know."

"Maybe it's time to move on."

"To what?"

"Your next object of fascination. Maybe you should ask Emily Vernon out."

"Emily?" As if it had never occurred to him — which it probably hadn't.

"Why not?"

Dennis digested that for a moment. "Why?" he said.

"It's just an idea," I said, shaking my head.

LITA

I was updating my blog when Emily called.

"I am dissolving," she said.

"Too much bubble bath?"

"Angst. Angst and ennui. I may be entirely dissipated by morning."

"Have you been reading *The Bell Jar* again?"

"No. *Wuthering Heights*. My bones are jelly."

"Oh dear. A cappuccino might help resolidify you. Do your bones have enough strength left in them to get you to Starbucks?"

• • •

Emily beat me to Starbucks by half a venti cappuccino. She may have been dissipated but she had a solid caffeine buzz going. I ordered a latte with a shot of hazelnut and joined her at the back table.

"I am giving up on Dennis Long," she said. "I am swearing off all men for at least ten years."

"What about after that?"

"I will be ancient and creaky, and I may need a man to take out the trash."

"I can see you've thought this out."

"I may get a motorcycle and a mud-flap haircut."

"You're switching teams?"

"Yes. I am going to become a lesbian biker."

Much as I liked the idea of having a lesbian biker friend, I couldn't see Emily in that role.

"How about we give Dennis one more try?" I said.

"How?"

"All we have to do is make sure he understands how hot you are."

"I can be hot?"

"You can be scorching. You already have the shoes. You —"

"Hey, guys!" It was Tracy Spink and Erica Smith.

"Hi, Tracy," said Emily.

"Did you hear about Dennis and Blair?" Tracy said.

My stomach flip-flopped. I'd have bet that Emily's did the same thing, although we were both expecting very different news. We shook our heads.

Tracy looked ready to burst with the need to share some hot gossip, but Erica beat her to the punch.

"Blair went totally postal on him," she said. "She hit him! Right in front of the school!"

"Why did she do that?" Emily asked.

Erica and Tracy looked at each other and performed a synchronized shrug.

"She was yelling something about rabbits," Tracy said.

Chapter Seventeen
BRETT REDUX

Hi, Miz Fitz,

What do you think of playing hard to get?

— Elusive

Miz Fitz sez:

It's no game.

ADAM

Miz Fitz's Top Ten Things turned out to be just the beginning. Her blog contained page after page of questions and answers about guys and girls. All I had to do was copy, paste, and change a few words here and there to make it sound more like me and less like Miz Fitz. Mostly it was a matter of making it less snarky, like changing *Most boys have the emotional depth of earthworms* to *Some guys have trouble understanding what girls want.*

By Friday morning, I had nearly fifty pages.

I needed to talk to somebody, so I stayed after class to talk to Ms. Ling.

"I'm writing a book," I said.

"Adam," she said. "I am so impressed!"

"It's the story of my life. So far it's nine hundred pages long. Will you read it?"

Her mouth fell open, then closed into a painful-looking smile. "Nine . . . hundred?"

"Just kidding," I said.

"You aren't really writing a book?"

"Oh, I'm writing a book. But it will only be about a hundred pages."

She smiled again, this time with less uncertainty. "Is it a novel?"

"It's a self-help book."

"Really! Who are you helping?"

"Girls. It's about why boys act the way they do."

"Sounds like a bestseller! Do you have a publisher?"

"I'm self-publishing."

"That's very ambitious. Do you have an editor?"

"I don't need an editor — I'm *self*-publishing."

"You'll still need someone to check for grammar, spelling, and so forth."

"Maybe you could do that. You know, as part of your job?"

She looked startled, then shook her head slowly. "Adam, I don't really think I'm qualified to edit your manuscript, but I'd be happy to take a look at it when you've finished."

"Great! Thanks! Um . . . will I get extra credit?"

Ms. Ling laughed.

LITA

Another Anger Walk. This time I was mad at Adam (on general principles), at my dad (because he was in LA and unable to defend himself), at Emily (for being such a wimp), and at myself. Why me? Because I should've been able to let all that crap roll off me, and because it bothered me that I cared, and because I was sick of being sixteen years old, and because I felt guilty about getting Dennis slapped. And that made me mad at Dennis for not ducking and at myself all over again because why should I let it bother me? Dennis deserved to get slapped, if not for what Blair thought he'd done, then certainly for being oblivious to Emily.

It was cool outside, cloudy and gusty in that threatening early fall way that makes you start thinking about gloves. I had my fists jammed in the pockets of my hoodie, and I was walking so hard that every step sent a shock wave up my spine to the base of my brain. My eyes were fixed on the sidewalk a few feet in front of me, and I was paying little attention to where I was or where I was going, when suddenly before me on the sidewalk was a pair of booted feet sticking out from beneath a car.

I once read that everything we do is intentional. You hit your thumb with a hammer, it's because you want to punish yourself. You eat too much, it's because you want to hide beneath a layer of flab. You say something incredibly embarrassing, it's because it needed to be said.

Frankly, I've never believed any of that. I believe in accidents pure and simple. I don't want to be responsible for every stupid thing I do or say and there was No Way I had intentionally returned to the domain of Brett the grease monkey.

No Way.

"Hey," I said, giving the nearest foot a little kick. "Blocking traffic again."

Brett slid out from under the car.

"So walk around, little girl." He grinned, taking a bit of the sting out of "little girl." Not that I cared.

"I thought you had this piece of junk fixed. Didn't I see you at the bakery?"

"That was you?" He sat up. "Were you the bear claw or the sprinkle doughnut?"

"Sprinkle."

"Kind of hard to recognize you with the hoodie and the shades."

I lowered my sunglasses and raised one eyebrow, giving him my Mr. Spock look.

He laughed. Nice laugh for a dropout grease monkey.

"And how are things at Harvard, Emma Woodhouse?"

"It's *Ms.* Woodhouse to you."

"My apologies, Ms. Woodhouse."

"*Apologies?* That's a whole four syllables. I'm impressed!"

"I've got lots of them. Watch." He took a breath. "Convertible. Radiator. Speedometer. Overhead cam —"

"Overhead cam is two words."

"Oh. Hey, you got a minute?"

"No."

"I need you to crank this thing while I look at the starter motor."

"What does 'crank this thing' mean?"

"Turn the key. It'll just take a second. Please."

I shrugged, tried to come up with a good reason to refuse him, failed to do so, and got in the car.

"Wait till I say go!" he shouted as he wriggled his way underneath.

"What if it starts and I run over you?"

"Don't put it in gear! Give me a couple seconds."

I looked around the interior of the car. Typical boy stuff — empty bakery bag, Coke cans, a car magazine, a stinky air freshener shaped like a pine tree, a pair of beat-up Nikes (the air freshener did not quite cancel them out), and a paperback copy of *Pride and Prejudice*.

I closed my eyes, then opened them. *Pride and Prejudice* was still sitting on the passenger seat.

I thought, *Waitaminute . . . he reads Jane Austen?* Then I came to my senses and saw it for what it was. A clue — as in: time-to-get-one, girl. Obviously, this car jockey had a semiliterate girlfriend.

I realized that he was shouting something. I stuck my head out the window.

"What?"

"I said, *Turn the key!*"

"Okay, okay!" I turned the key but my heart wasn't in it.

Chapter Eighteen
ASSUMPTIONS

Dear Miz Fitz,

My boyfriend thinks I am a very suspicious person. I think there is something he is not telling me.

— Gwendolyn

Miz Fitz sez:

I agree with both of you.

ADAM

Since I was half done with the book, I figured I'd devote my weekend to some serious marketing. I had already taken orders for thirty books just by talking to kids I knew at school, but that was just scratching the surface. There were plenty of kids I didn't know, and a lot of other schools.

I went to work on a flyer:

WHAT BOYS WANT

The **TRUTH** about what **REAL BOYS** are
THINKING, SAYING, and **DOING**

when it comes to

SEX, LOVE, and ROMANTCE!

This is **NOT** some hard-to-read scholarly text written by some professor with bifocals and a paunch. **WHAT BOYS WANT** is written by a **REAL** teenage boy, and it contains the **REAL FACTS**. You want straight talk about what goes on in boys' heads?

YOU NEED THIS BOOK!!!!

TRUE FACTS • NO TABOOS

STATISFACTION GUARANTEED

WHAT BOYS WANT answers **ALL** of the questions they **REFUSE TO ANSWER** in **HEATH CLASS**, including:

- What's the sexiest part of a gril? (Hint: It's not breasts!!!)
- Boners — What causes them, and how often do boys get them?
- How much time do boys *REALLY* spend thinking about sex?
- How many boys have *REALLY* gone all the way?
- The Skank Factor: Do dirty girls *REALLY* get the guys?

Order your copy today — **ONLY $10.00!!!!!**
(after October 15, the price will increase to $15.00)

It looked great!

I added my email address and phone number to the bottom of the flyer, printed it out, then drove it over to the Repo Man Copy Shop. At first I was going to order a thousand copies. I figured I could distribute them at school and at other high schools in the area — maybe go to events like swim meets, and girls' basketball and soccer games. The more I thought about it, a thousand flyers wouldn't be nearly enough, so I ordered five thousand. That put a pretty scary dent in my meager financial reserves.

The guy at Repo Man told me I couldn't pick up my flyers until Thursday — something to do with the special paper I'd ordered — so I went over to Dennis's house to see if Blair had left any fingerprints on his face.

His father answered the door.

"Adam. It's a beautiful day, isn't it?"

I hadn't really noticed the weather, but Mr. Long was into that sort of thing.

"I guess so," I said, looking up at the bright blue sky for the first time that day.

"Not many days like this left. Another month or so and we'll be looking at snow." Always with the weather. "I suppose you're looking for Dennis."

"Is he home?"

"He's hiding out in his boy-cave. Why don't you see if you can coax him out into the sunshine."

"I'll do my best," I said.

Dennis's "boy-cave" was his bedroom, a tangled mass of electronic equipment, dirty clothes, and books. Dennis was glued to his computer, working some game that involved screeching robot dinosaurs and explosions that tested the limits of his tiny desktop speakers.

"Hang on a sec," he said. A rapid series of electronic explosions followed. He smiled, logged off, and looked up at me. "What's up?"

"Just so there's no confusion," I said, "I'm a real person."

"Too bad. If you were virtual, I'd give you a grenade launcher, some cool armor, and a half-naked Amazon girl."

"Speaking of half-naked Amazonians, how's your face?"

Dennis put a hand to his left cheek.

"No permanent damage," he said. "But I'm still trying to figure out why she hit me. Hey! Why don't *you* ask her?"

"She might hit me, too."

"She likes you."

"What makes you think that?"

Dennis shrugged. "I might be stupid about girls, but I'm not blind. The whole time we were talking in the hall the other day? You and me and Blair? She kept looking at you."

"Me?"

"You."

"Oh. Well, she's not my type. Don't worry."

"I didn't say I was worried."

We looked at each other for a beat, then — by mutual, unspoken agreement — dropped the subject so fast and hard you could almost hear it hit the floor.

LITA

The next several days of school faded into each other. Same classes, same faces, same behavior. The excitement and novelty of the first week, all those familiar faces with their summer tans, the new clothes, new facial hair, new classes . . . even the smell of the school building was interesting. But by week two, realizing that there were nearly forty weeks to go, we all slipped into an academic coma.

Not that *nothing* happened. Emily and I worked on her image. Knowing that Dennis had a thing for Blair, I coaxed Emily into some tight, leathery items. The effect was decidedly not Blair-like, but Emily was desperate enough to try anything. Dennis, oblivious, sank into a nerdy funk, devoting all of his energy to his classes. Emily could have been reborn as the goddess Venus, and Dennis would have mistaken her for a lamppost. I knew I had to get them one-on-one in an environment with no distractions, but I was coming up blank.

Blair strutted the halls, tossing her streaky hair, my dad stayed in LA, my mom continued to hammer away at her novel, and so on. The only notable events — or nonevents, to be precise — were that I did not see the dropout mechanic again, Mrs. Crowe remained absent from her job at the library, the *New Yorker* did not publish any of my poems, and my sucky novel remained cowering in its drawer.

Usually, I could have relied on Adam for entertainment — coffee drinks after school, a good, long phone conversation, or a movie. Adam was the only guy I knew who actually liked romantic comedies. But these days he was all about his "book." It was all he talked about. Also, his incessant good nature was getting on my nerves. You know how it is when you're enjoying a good funk and somebody tells you to have a nice day? I didn't need his happy face messing with my clinical depression.

I decided it was easiest to go cold turkey and simply not speak to him. I didn't need Adam. I didn't need anybody. Still, I missed his goofy smile, like there was this hole in my life.

I spent the next several evenings doing homework and blogging. Every now and then I thought about Brett and thanked God I didn't have a thing for him like Emily had for Dennis. It would have been unbearably awkward, him with a Jane Austen–reading girlfriend already, not to mention the fact that he was a grease monkey.

I made it through most of the week without cracking a smile. Problem was, it's no fun being a wet blanket all by yourself. By Thursday night, I was totally caught up on homework, there was nothing on TV, my mom was completely buried in her book, Emily was babysitting her cousins, and I was sick to death of sitting in front of my computer.

Pathetic? Absolutely. Here I was trying so hard to get Emily hooked up with Dennis while my own social life was in the toilet.

Usually, when I'm feeling like a loser, I think about other people who are even worse losers. Like Emily and Dennis. Or Blair Thompson, trapped inside her own skanky self. Or Mrs. Crowe the hyper-conservative fanatic. I wondered what she was doing. Sitting in a courthouse in Reno waiting for her divorce papers? Or maybe she was home. Once again I felt a thought I'd been avoiding come slithering out from my guilt box and tickle my consciousness.

What if Mrs. Crowe's divorce was partly my fault?

It was entirely possible. The great Viagra and Ex-Lax scandal would never have occurred but for *moi*.

I went to my closet and put on my black cotton trench coat, my black floppy hat, and my speediest pair of sneakers. Since my own life sucked, I would amuse myself by prying into the affairs of others. Slipping out of the house into the night, quiet and dark as a shadow, I headed east on Colson Boulevard.

Chapter Nineteen
THE OTHER WOMAN

Q: Why do boys do things that are dangerous?

A: Boys perform dangerous acts because it's fun and exciting, and because they do not believe they can die.

— **from** *What Boys Want*

LITA

The Crowes lived in a neighborhood of small, boxlike houses a few blocks from Wellstone High. They had a well-kept yard and a separate garage, behind which were two small plastic trash cans, one for trash and one for recycling. Very convenient. But on this night I was not interested in garbage. Instead, I stood quietly and nearly invisibly in my trench coat on the sidewalk where I could see through the open shades into the living room. A flickering light indicated the presence of a television. Someone was home.

Had Mrs. Crowe returned from her visit to Nevada? I moved in closer, angling to see what was on the TV.

A human hand, severed at the wrist, on a stainless-steel tray. They must be watching *CSI*. Staying in the shadows, I moved to the left until I could see who was watching.

At the far end of a worn leather sofa, I saw a woman's bare feet and legs flopped across a man's lap. The man was Mr. Crowe (a nice-looking guy, except for being half bald) wearing blue jeans and a Harrah's Casino T-shirt. But who owned the legs? I sidled up to the window and got my face right next to the glass. A potted philodendron blocked my view. They could have been Mrs. Crowe's legs — or the legs of Another Woman.

Either way, this was good news. I had been worried that my dumpster diving of last spring had triggered their divorce, but if they were cuddled up together on the sofa, then the divorce had never happened. Or if those weren't Mrs. Crowe's legs, then there was Another Woman, which also let me off the hook — if they broke up because Mr. Crowe was having an affair, then it wasn't my fault.

"Yes!" I whispered to myself. But I still wanted to know who the woman was, so I waited. Every twenty seconds or so Mr. Crowe would take a chip from a bowl on the end table and put it in his mouth.

A few minutes later, I heard a faint ringing. Mr. Crowe picked up the telephone from the end table and spoke for a few seconds. After he hung up, he said something to the woman, lifted her legs from his lap, and went through a door that I figured must lead to the kitchen.

Get up! I projected my will at the woman on the sofa. *Move to where I can see you!*

She didn't move. I waited. Then I heard the soft sound of footsteps on grass, very close. My heart stopped completely. I turned my head to look directly into the angry features of Mr. Harold Crowe.

"You're a girl," he said, his voice tight.

My heart started beating again with huge throat-swelling thumps. I nodded.

"You're lucky," he said. "If you were a guy, you'd be laid out on the grass right now with a bloody nose."

I took off running. I'd made it almost to the sidewalk when I felt him grab the back of my coat. I spun, going for the midair kung-fu kick — not that I had any idea how to perform such a maneuver — but the tail of my trench coat wrapped around my legs and I went down like a sack of potatoes.

Mr. Crowe stood over me. "Are you okay?" he asked.

I sat up and nodded.

From across the street, a man yelled, "Everything all right over there, Harry?"

"I've got it under control," Mr. Crowe replied. "Thanks for the call!"

"No problem. We like to keep an eye out." The neighbor went back into his house.

Mr. Crowe, looking down and shaking his head, said, "I bet you're the one who went through our garbage last April."

I tried lying. "No! I just . . ." I just what? I was so busted, I was Humpty Dumpty. "I just . . . Mrs. Crowe — your wife — hasn't been at school, and I was walking by, and I just wondered if everything was, you know, okay?"

He squatted down so that his face was hanging right over me. His breath smelled of Doritos.

"Why wouldn't things be okay?"

"So . . . that's Mrs. Crowe in there?"

"Who else would it be?" he said, looking puzzled.

"I heard you were getting divorced."

"Who did you hear *that* from?"

"I don't know. I just heard it."

Mr. Crowe expelled a gust of air through his nostrils. "You kids jump to conclusions like fleas to a dog."

"I'm sorry."

"I know who you are," he said. "Cory pointed you out to me one time. Your name is Lita, right? The girl who wanted to check out *Lady Chatterley's Lover*."

I couldn't deny it. "The school library didn't have it," I said. "Can you believe it? A famous book like that?"

He laughed and sat back on his heels. "Did you ever find a copy?"

"Yes, at the public library. It was mostly pretty boring."

"That's what I thought, too." He pressed his lips tight together, then said, "What am I going to do with you?"

"How about nothing?"

"I don't want to get Cory all worked up. She's *still* upset over your little garbage raid." He looked back at the house. "If I let you go, will you promise to not do this anymore?"

"Okay."

He stood up. "I'd better get back before Cory comes looking for me. This is the last thing she needs." He jabbed his forefinger at me. "And you be nice to her at school, okay?"

"I promise," I said as I climbed to my feet.

"One more thing," he said. "Not that it's any of your business, but that Viagra and Ex-Lax you found? That was my uncle's. He died last spring. We were just getting rid of some of his stuff."

Chapter Twenty
THE TUTOR TRAP (PART 1)

Dear Miz Fitz,

The boy I like is always with a bunch of his creepy friends, which makes him act creepy, too. How can I get him alone?

— LionessRoar

The Predatory Miz Fitz sez:

Like dogs, boys travel in packs. It is an ancient defense mechanism, and difficult to overcome. My recommendation is to follow the pack day and night, taking care to remain under-cover, until you see him go off on his own. Then pounce.

LITA

I found Adam in the school library of all places, sitting at one of the study tables, typing something into his laptop.

"Hey," I said. "I'm speaking to you again."

He looked up. "Were we not speaking?"

"Yes, earthworm, we haven't spoken for days."

"I *thought* it was quiet around here." He grinned.

I said, "I wanted to let you know that the Crowes are still married. You should really be more careful about spreading rumors like that."

"I didn't spread any rumors! I just told you what books Mrs. Crowe was looking at!"

"That's how rumors start."

"Well, I didn't *spread* it. Talking to you isn't *spreading*. It's just talking to you. You're not everyone else."

I didn't say anything to that. He had a point.

"So how come you weren't talking to me?" he asked.

"I just figured you were too busy. With your book and all."

He didn't get that I was being a little sarcastic. "I *have* been busy," he said. "I have a new marketing strategy. I'm going to distribute flyers."

I couldn't help myself. "That's not very original," I said.

"It's the *way* I'm distributing them. You'll see."

"I'm sure I will." Just then I noticed Robbie Conseco a few tables back reading a book. "Is that *Robbie*?" I asked. "Reading a *book*? Since when does Robbie *read*?"

Adam looked over at Robbie. "He got such crappy grades last year his folks hired a tutor for him, some grad student from the college. He's got Robbie doing all kinds of extra reading."

"Tutor?" An idea blossomed.

"Yeah . . . Lita? Are you okay?"

"I'm better than okay," I said. "I'm perfect. Do you think Dennis would be interested in making some money?"

"I know he's saving up for a new game system."

"I was thinking he might be a good science tutor."

Adam looked at me and raised an eyebrow.

"For Emily," I said.

ADAM

Miss Morris kicked me out of the library at four. I took my briefcase and walked down the hall, testing each classroom door as I passed. The third door opened. I slipped inside, closed the door behind me, and locked it.

Judging from the maps, globes, and travel posters, I was in a geography classroom. I could have done worse. At least there were some magazines to look at. I could have ended up stuck in an algebra classroom.

I settled into the teacher's comfortable chair with my feet up on the desk and a stack of *National Geographics*. I had a long wait ahead of me.

High school after hours is one of the quietest places I've ever been. At first, there was the distant sound of voices, and an occasional clanging or clunking or hissing, but by six o'clock, when the hallway lights went out and the last of the after-school club members, detention regulars, faculty, and maintenance staff were gone, the silence became utter and complete.

Just to be safe, I waited another half hour, then crept out into the hallway. I kicked my shoes off and ran silently past the library, up the steps, and down the hall to the office. Nobody there. I went down to the maintenance room and pushed the door open a crack. No light, no sound. The janitors had left for the day.

I was alone.

Time to get to work.

"But I'm doing fine in biology," Emily said to me that night, over at my house. "I mean, it's kind of gross sometimes, but it's not that hard. I'll get a B without half trying."

"Yeah, but with a tutor you could get an A *and* a D. D as in Dennis."

She wasn't getting it.

"Look," I said, "Dennis needs money —"

"Who doesn't?"

"— and you need Dennis."

Her mouth opened in sudden comprehension. Then it closed.

"It's brilliant," I said. "Remember last year when you were having algebra troubles, and your parents offered to hire a tutor for you? I think you should start having difficulties with biology."

Emily gave that a moment's thought, then shook her head. "Wouldn't that be like paying him to be with me?"

"It wouldn't be you paying. It would be your mom and dad."

"Still, it seems weird." She thought some more. I could almost see the wheels turning.

I said, "When a boy asks you out on a date, he pays, right? What's the difference?"

"It feels different," she said, but I could see her coming around.

"I can talk to him if you want. Set it up."

Emily looked at her feet. She was wearing her ridiculous heels again.

"What do you think he would charge?" she asked.

Chapter Twenty-one
BUSTED

Dear Miz Fitz,

I like this guy, but then one of my girlfriends heard from her friend that a friend of the guy I like said that the guy was going around saying that I said I was his girlfriend or something, which is totally not true. How can I let him know that I never said what he is saying I said without making him think that I don't want to go out with him?

— Hermione

Miz Fitz sez:

One moment, please — you have given Miz Fitz the whirlies . . .

. . . okay, I think you are saying your problem is too many friends saying too many things to too many people. Why don't you just ask him out?

ADAM

One thousand six-hundred forty student lockers lined the halls of Wellstone High. Each locker had four vent slits near the top. I had to fold each fluorescent orange flyer in half to fit it through. After the first ten minutes it was not fun anymore. I stopped and did the math. I had stuffed sixty lockers so far. At that rate, it would take me four and a half hours to stuff every locker in school.

My mom thought I was having dinner with Dennis. How long before she called Dennis's house to check up on me?

Not four and a half hours.

I quickly developed a system. Fold the flyers ten at a time, then stuff ten lockers. It went a little faster then, but I still wouldn't have time to finish and get home before my mom got on the phone. I wished I could tell the girls' lockers from the boys', but since that wasn't possible, I had to stuff them all.

The novelty of being alone in the school building soon wore off. It was getting dark outside, and with no lights on in the school, I could hardly see to get the flyers into the slits. And my hands were getting sore from all the creasing and stuffing. I was thinking about just doing a few hundred lockers, then going home — see what kind of response I got and come back another night if I got enough orders to make it worthwhile.

That was when I found out I was not alone.

"Busted!"

For half a second I thought the voice had come from inside my own head, then a bright light hit me from behind, and my heart

"With every kid in school looking at a bright orange flyer? He'll notice, all right."

"Freedom of speech," I said.

"Yeah, right. That'll go over real big with Graves." She shined the flashlight in my face again, "Tell me. How did I score?"

Oh crap, we were back to the Skank Scale. I thought fast, and decided it was time for a believable lie. "You averaged three point five," I said. "Just skanky enough to be interesting."

Blair nodded. Apparently, she found that acceptable. I figured it was time to change the subject again, so I repeated my earlier question.

"So, what are you doing here?"

She looked at me for a long time before answering.

"It's cheaper than a hotel," she said.

Chapter Twenty-two
HOTEL WELLSTONE

Q: How important is makeup to a guy?

A: I guess if a guy is willing to wear lipstick, it must be pretty important to him. But if you're talking about makeup for girls, I'd say it's about one tenth of one percent as important as having a friendly smile, nice hair, and good listening skills.

— **from** *What Boys Want*

ADAM

Sometimes you think you know somebody, and then you find out something about them, and *boom*, it's like they become a completely different person. Like when my uncle Gardner from California, the most boring and ordinary guy in the world — he's a corporate lawyer — told me that Snoop Dogg used to be his neighbor, and that they had smoked a bong together. I never saw my uncle the same after that.

When Blair told me she was using the school as a free hotel, I realized that I didn't actually know anything about her — not really.

"My mom's boyfriend is a jerk," she said. "When he's staying at our house, I find someplace else to be. It's just easier."

"Why? Is he violent or something?"

"No. It's just . . . my mom acts like a teenager when he's around. It's kind of disgusting."

"That's ugly, when parents start acting like us."

"No kidding." We laughed.

"Do you always stay here at school?"

"I have friends I stay with usually. But sometimes I like having all this space to myself. I can imagine I'm the only person left on the planet."

"Where do you sleep?"

"On the bed in the nurse's office. It's not bad. I get up and shower at about five, then make myself breakfast in the cafeteria kitchen. It's a very *skanky* way to live."

More with the skank stuff. Time to change the subject yet again.

"Are you still working at the Dairy Queen?"

"God, no. Who told you that?"

"Dennis said he saw you out there."

"That was just for the summer. I'll never eat a soft-serve cone again as long as I live."

"Uh . . . can I ask you something?"

She pointed the flashlight right in my eyes and waited.

"How come you went off on Dennis?"

She laughed. "'Cause he's a jerk?"

"He is?"

"Telling everybody I was all hot for his pudgy little bod?"

"He did?"

"That's what everybody was saying. So I went up to him and . . . I don't know, I was going to just yell at him, but then all of a sudden it was like I could imagine him telling people stuff about me that wasn't true, and . . . I guess I just needed to hit somebody. Not that he didn't deserve it. The twerp."

"I'm glad you don't need to hit somebody tonight."

"Not yet."

I said, "I don't think Dennis would say anything bad about you. Somebody must have got it wrong."

Blair shrugged as if it really didn't matter. "I've been wrong before," she said. She pointed her flashlight at my backpack full of flyers. "You planning on stuffing *all* the lockers?"

"I don't think I have time," I said. "I have to be home by nine or so."

"You want a hand?"

I did, but I was confused.

"Why would you want to help me if you think me and all my friends are jerks?"

"*You* might be salvageable." She thought for a moment, then said, "Everybody makes mistakes."

We took turns folding and stuffing, talking the whole time.

Blair asked, "What made you want to write a book?"

"It was kind of a market-driven thing. I thought of a book that people would buy, so I decided to write it. I'm about a third done."

"You're kind of compulsive, aren't you?"

"I guess. Oh, and guess where I got the idea for stuffing these lockers. From Graves — that notice we all got in our lockers the first day of school?"

"Will that be your defense when he busts you?"

"It's worth a try."

A little later — I was getting tired — I said, "So what's with all the black?"

"All the black what?"

"You know — how you dress. All in black and red." She was wearing black leather pants and a tight, black tank top that showed about two inches of belly. Her feet were bare, but earlier that day she'd been wearing black engineer boots.

"Why? Too *skanky* for you?"

"No! I was just asking."

"I like black. It feels right."

"I like you without your makeup."

"That's because you have an undeveloped sense of style. I mean, *look* at you!"

I looked down. Untucked, short-sleeved, green-and-yellow-checked cotton shirt. Jeans. Basketball shoes, well broken in.

"I'm not goth, that's for sure," I said.

"You think *I'm* goth?"

"If you're not goth, what are you?"

"I'm unclassifiable."

"I think you look good," I said.

She stuffed a few more lockers without saying anything.

I said, "I mean, I'm not that into clothes. You'd probably look good no matter how you dressed."

"Even if I dressed like a skank?"

"You aren't going to let up with that, are you?"

"Why should I? I like it when you blush."

"I'm not blushing. Even if I was, it's too dark in here for you to see."

"I can see in the dark. Like a cat."

It was after eight o'clock, and we still had about five hundred lockers to go. I was getting a blister on my thumb from creasing flyers.

"I have to get home pretty soon," I said.

"If you want, I can finish up. I don't have anything else to do tonight."

"You'd really do that?"

"I'll expect a free copy of your book."

"Deal."

It felt awkward saying good-bye. I had the feeling I should touch her somehow, but I also got the feeling that if I put my hand on her arm she'd slap it away. And shaking hands would seem just too stiff and formal. In the end, I just said, "see ya!" and "thanks!" about five different times, let myself out through a classroom window, and headed for home.

Chapter Twenty-three
THE TERMINATOR

Miz Fitz,

Is it true that you can tell how big a boy's thing is from his shoe size?

— Up All Night Wondering

Miz Fitz sez:

If by "thing" you mean "foot," then the answer is yes.

LITA

Mr. Crowe had implied that he wouldn't mention my little escapade to Mrs. Crowe, but I didn't believe him. Married people are notoriously bad at keeping secrets from each other. And if Mr. Crowe told her about me being the window peeper and dumpster diver, Mrs. Crowe was exactly the sort of priss-butt to take that information directly to Principal Graves, who would probably have me staked out on an anthill.

I decided to avoid the library for . . . oh, say, the rest of my life.

Which was too bad because it was my favorite place in the whole school. Fortunately, I ran into Emily first thing Monday morning, which meant I could wallow in her problems instead of my own.

"I changed my mind," she said. "No tutor."

"Too late," I said. "I already talked to him."

"You didn't!"

The truth was, I hadn't. But if you can't lie to your best friend for her own good, who *can* you lie to?

"It's done," I said.

"Oh." She tried to fake a frown but didn't look all *that* unhappy about it.

We were walking toward our lockers to unload unnecessary books and stuff when I noticed dozens of sheets of bright orange paper littering the hallway. I heard laughter from a cluster of sophomore boys who were all looking at one of the sheets.

One of them shouted, "I got a boner! I got a boner!"

Which is a really strange thing for a sophomore to be yelling in the school hallway at 7:40 A.M.

The other boys collapsed into hysterical laughter.

"What's *that* about?" Emily asked as she spun the combination on her locker.

"I have no idea."

She opened her locker door and one of the orange sheets fell out onto the floor. I snatched it up and started reading.

"What is it?" Emily said, trying to grab it away from me.

"Oh. My. God," I said.

ADAM

Thirty-six pages.

That was how many pages I wrote over the weekend. Of course, most of it was stuff I borrowed from Miz Fitz, then changed a little bit. But still — *thirty-six pages*! My book was up to eighty-six pages and I'd been working on it less than two weeks.

I was so impressed with myself that I almost forgot about the flyers — until I stepped into the school and saw them littering the hallway floors.

This would not go unnoticed.

LITA

I had to admit, Adam's marketing strategy was getting a lot of attention. All anybody was talking about was those flyers: *How did he get them into the lockers? What would the book be like? Are you gonna buy one?* Neon-orange paper airplanes were sailing through every classroom. Neon-orange flyers with tons of typos. Why didn't he ask me to check his spelling before he printed them? Not that I cared about him and his stupid book. I had projects of my own. Like Dennis and Emily.

I didn't get a chance to talk to Dennis until third period. First thing he said to me was, "So how about Adam's flyer?"

"Forget his stupid flyer," I said. "Do you still need money to buy that PlayBox or whatever?"

"Uh . . . yeah?"

"How does fifteen bucks an hour sound? Three hours a week."

Dennis did the math. He was good at that.

ADAM

My first three classes, I expected the tap on the shoulder to come at any moment. Instead, I took twenty-two more book orders and got several amused looks from my teachers. And I sweated a lot.

I saw Blair only once, walking with Dahlia, going the opposite way down the hall. She was back to her usual self, hidden behind a mask of makeup. I smiled and nodded as we passed each other, but she completely ignored me. Or maybe she was so busy talking to Dahlia she didn't see me.

The tap came as I was going to lunch. It wasn't really a tap, though. It was more like a vise grip on my upper arm.

"Let's go, Merchant." It was Vice Principal Marianne Berman, aka the Terminator.

Chapter Twenty-four
FOURTEEN MILLION

Q: What do boys want more — sex or love?

A: Most boys would probably answer "sex," but that is only because they never get any. For the real answer, go google the word sex. *You will get a couple billion hits. Now google the word* love. *You will get four times as many.*

— **from** *What Boys Want*

ADAM

Principal Graves made me sit in front of his desk while he worked on a Rubik's Cube. The Terminator stood silently behind me with her arms crossed over her formidable bosom. In case I made a break for it, I guess.

I spent the next minute or so watching Graves fumble with the cube while I pondered the difference between "bosom" and "boobs." Maybe they were "boobs" when you could tell there were two of them, and a "bosom" when the two boobs grew together to form a single shelflike protuberance.

Graves had the cube almost solved, but he was missing a key move. I could hear faint grunts and exhalations coming from his tightly closed mouth. Finally, he tossed the cube on his desk.

"Confiscated from one of our sophomores," he said. "It relaxes me."

He did not look relaxed.

"Do you want me to show you?" I said, indicating the cube. I could have solved it in five or six twists.

"No, I do not," he said.

Bob Glaus had once compared Principal Graves with Rick Moranis — the guy who shrunk his kids in that old movie — because they both wore the same kind of glasses. I thought he looked more like a younger, beardless Santa Claus: heavy, balding, and jolly on the surface. But there was no jolliness that day.

He leaned forward as far as he could, desktop digging into his belly, and stabbed a pudgy finger at me.

"Let's cut to the chase, Merchant. And if the words *freedom of speech* emerge from your mouth even one time, I will have you permanently and irrevocably expelled from Wellstone High. Do you understand me?"

He had made the first move, and what a move it was! My entire defense, undermined with one sentence. They must teach that in principal school.

"This," he said, holding a crumpled orange flyer in his fist, "is unacceptable. This school is not your little marketing laboratory. And this book you are attempting to promote is decidedly *not* a part of our curriculum."

I opened my mouth to speak, but Graves held up a hand. "I do not know how or when you stuffed this junk mail into the school lockers.

Frankly, I do not want to know. What I do want from you is your promise to cease and desist from selling your book on campus or during school-related events. You will not speak of the book, you will not bring a copy onto school property, and you will not distribute any more flyers or other promotional materials."

He stopped for breath.

I tried to speak again, but he cut me off.

"I am disappointed in you, Adam."

"I'm sorry," I said, because when speaking to angry adults, that's the best way to start out. "Maybe selling the book in school wasn't such a good idea" — actually, I still thought it was a *great* idea — "but I didn't think you'd mind."

"Really." Graves was giving me a cocked eyebrow, this-is-gonna-be-good look. "And why did you think that?"

"Because the book is partly for my creative writing class. Ms. Ling is giving me extra credit. Also, I was just following your example."

He sat back and raised both eyebrows, a very comical look on Graves — there was about three inches of brow between his eyebrows and the tops of his glasses.

"Remember that note you left in everybody's locker the first day of school?" I said. "I just thought that was a really good idea."

I noticed that Graves was getting a little red in the neck. That should have clued me to shut up, but for some reason I kept talking.

"I mean, it's very efficient if you think about it, and cheaper than TV advertising. And since I got the idea from you, I thought —"

"Merchant! Shut up!"

I shut up. Graves's face had turned a scary shade of pink, and suddenly I remembered what Blair had said.

Graves is gonna pop a vessel.

LITA

I lined up Dennis and Emily for a Wednesday night tutoring session, and I managed to avoid running into Mrs. Crowe. I should have left school at the end of the day feeling pretty good, but instead I felt extremely schlumpish. Lita Wold, teenage schlump.

What is a schlump, anyway? When I got home I typed it into my dictionary program and came up with "slow, slovenly, or inept person." That didn't quite fit. "Deprived" would be more accurate. Deprived of what? Well, all my friends had something exciting going on. Emily and Dennis were in love (with different people, but still . . .), Adam was doing his book thing, my dad was still in LA, my mother was sunk so deep into her novel she probably thought I was a wraith, and I was . . . what? All I had was my stupid blog and my utter mortification over the incident with Mr. Crowe.

Time for another Anger Walk. Or Deprivation Walk, which was pretty much the same thing. I put on my hoodie and took off, but as soon as I hit the sidewalk I realized I had a problem. I really did not want to deal with the dropout car jockey again, and it pissed me off that because of *him* I had to turn left, not right. I stood on the sidewalk fuming. I *hate* having my options limited. I pushed out my jaw (what my mother calls my stubborn two-year-old look) and decided I'd walk wherever I wanted to walk.

I turned right. But when I got to Holden Avenue there were no legs blocking the sidewalk. Instead of a gray car, the short driveway was filled with the cab end of a semi.

I slowed down as I walked past the house. Had Brett traded in his "classic" car for a truck? I walked around the truck and looked into the open garage. It was typical guy space, orderly and filthy all at the same time. A radio propped on a workbench was playing country-western music. I noticed several books piled on one end of the bench. Books draw me like a magnet. I had to see what they were. I stepped into the garage, close enough to read some of the titles: *The Great Gatsby, Invisible Man, Huckleberry Finn* — all older classics, and not what I expected to find on a workbench.

"Something I can do for you, son?"

I whirled around. An older man, probably in his forties, stood in front of the truck's huge grille, wiping his oily hands with a blue cloth. He had long, thinning, reddish hair gathered into a pathetic ponytail.

"Oh, hey, you're a girl. One of Brett's little sweeties, eh?"

Brett's little sweeties?

"Not hardly," I said. I started to move out of the garage, keeping as much space as possible between us, which wasn't much. He kept watching me with this moronic grin. He didn't strike me as particularly dangerous, but I didn't like being in that garage with him standing in the doorway. I hoped he wasn't Brett's dad.

He said, "If you aren't a friend of Brett's, then what are you doing in here?"

142

"I *know* Brett," I said. "That doesn't make me his sweetie."

The man threw back his head and roared. When he had finished laughing he said, "Tough little cookie, aren't you?" He ducked his head and peered beneath my hood. "Cute, too. What's your name, honey?"

"Elizabeth Bennet," I said, moving to get past him and out of the garage.

He made a quick move to his right, not enough to block me, but almost. I think he did it just to scare me. It did.

"Excuse me," I said.

He swept his arm out and performed a mocking bow. I walked quickly past him staying as far from that arm as possible.

"Don't be a stranger," he called after me.

ADAM

In a good news–bad news situation, I always like to start off with the good, because you never know when you're going to get struck by a stray meteorite, so you should always enjoy the good things while you can. Also, if you put off the bad things long enough you might never have to deal with them.

That's my theory, anyway.

The good news was that Graves's head had not exploded — at least not physically — and I'd sold lots of copies of my book. Plus, I had a whole week ahead of me with nothing to do but finish writing it.

The bad news? Five-day suspension. My parents would not be happy. Mostly my folks were cool, but me getting kicked out of school would definitely heat them up. So I came up with a plan: I would spend the rest of the week with my laptop at the public library. They would never know I wasn't at school, at least until Graves notified them. He had already called once and left a voice-mail message — fortunately, both my parents had been at work. I deleted it as soon as I got home. He would probably follow it up with an official letter, something like *Your evil son has been banished. Sign here.*

I could intercept the mail, but if he called them at work or on their cells, I'd be dead.

I called Lita to tell her what had happened.

Instead of "hello," she answered by saying, "I hear you got kicked out for littering."

"That's what I called to tell you."

"Three typos."

"What?"

"You had three typos in your flyer."

"Gimme a break. I'm dyslexic."

"No, you're not. You're just lazy."

This was not going well. I'd called looking for some sympathy.

"I thought you were done being mad at me."

"I'm not *mad*."

Which meant, of course, that she was. This called for a change of subject.

"How's the Emily and Dennis project going?" I asked.

"Very well, no thanks to you."

"Me? What did I do?"

"Nothing. Beep-beep!"

"Beep-beep?"

"That's the sound of my battery running low."

"Oh. It sounded like you saying 'Beep-beep.' I —"

She was gone. Had she hung up on me? I thought maybe she had. Oh well, I could call her tomorrow and apologize for whatever it was I'd done.

In the meantime, I had a book to write. I woke up my computer, opened Google, typed in the word *boner*, and got forty million hits.

Chapter Twenty-five
THE TUTOR TRAP (PART 2)

Boys and girls have different tastes in liquid refreshment. Girls prefer lightly carbonated waters in flavors such as raspberry, lemon, and kiwi, with or without sugar. Boys prefer Red Bull or beer. Only iced tea, cola, and coffee (the Holy Trinity of caffeine) may be safely served to either sex.

— **from** *What Boys Want*

LITA

The next morning I felt a little bad about my conversation with Adam, but not bad enough to call him. Besides, he'd probably forgotten about it thirty seconds after I hung up on him. Anyway, I was busy fretting about Emily and Dennis. Their first tutoring session had not gone as well as I had hoped.

"He was very serious," she said, "and not much of a tutor. He spent most of the time reading me things out of our biology book."

"Did you feed him?"

"I made nachos."

"Nachos are good. And to drink?"

"Fizzy water. Raspberry. It was all we had."

"Hmm."

"I couldn't believe how much he ate. Anyway, at one point he told me I was really smart. He said he didn't think I needed a tutor."

"What did you say?"

"I told him to close his mouth."

I looked at her.

"He leaves his mouth hanging open all the time. I told him to close it."

"Did it work?"

"He pretty much kept it closed after that, except when he was talking or stuffing nachos in it."

"So he's trainable. That's good. What were you wearing?"

"T-shirt. My new jeans."

"Next time show him some cleavage."

"I don't think I *have* cleavage."

"You know what I mean. Make him notice your bod."

"You know what was the worst part? My dad looked in on us, like, six times."

"Dads like to do that."

"Yeah, but it's not like we were in my bedroom. We were in the *kitchen*. What did he think we were going to do? Get naked and do it on the stove? And here's the worst part. Dennis asks me, 'How come your dad keeps sticking his head in here?' And I say, 'He just wants to make sure you're not taking advantage of me.' You know what he says next?"

"Surprise me."

"He says, 'Why would I do that?'"

• • •

After talking to Emily, I was in desperate need of a good romantic novel, so I slipped into the library just after lunch, hoping Mrs. Crowe would still be on her break.

No such luck.

But it wasn't so bad. She was straightening books on the shelves and making little *tch* sounds whenever she found a book out of order. When she saw me, she just gave me her usual prim, disapproving nod.

Apparently, her husband hadn't mentioned my little visit. I set about scanning the fiction section, trolling for romance.

"Looking for anything in particular?" Mrs. Crowe asked.

"Something romantic," I said.

"Something along the lines of *Lady Chatterley's Lover*, I suppose?"

"Do you have it?"

The look she gave me then was all I needed to know. Mr. Crowe had blabbed.

Miss Morris must have overheard. She stepped between us and said, "How about *Rebecca*?"

Mrs. Crowe abruptly turned away and continued her straightening.

"*Rebecca* is Daphne du Maurier's greatest gothic romance," Miss Morris explained. She moved down the shelf and pulled out a well-read copy. "You will like this book," she said.

The great thing about Miss Morris is that every time she has ever said that to me, she's been right.

I read *Rebecca* all in one night. It was exactly what I needed: romance, mystery, spookiness, and an ending that didn't leave me feeling empty and awful. You know what I mean about books with empty endings? You get there and think, "Is that all?" The worst ones are the books that end up with everybody dead or miserable. Even though those books are probably the most realistic.

I don't read for reality. I've got enough of that. *Rebecca* was perfect.

At three A.M., I was on my computer in my Miz Fitz guise blogging about Daphne du Maurier. I knew I'd be toast in the morning but I could afford to zombie my way through one day.

It didn't take long for me to get blogged-out. My eyeballs were fried. The letters on the display were dancing around like little ants but I wasn't sleepy. You know how you get too tired to sleep? That was me. I got into my sleeping outfit (Pajamas, *no.* Ancient T-shirt and cotton gym shorts, *yes.*) and flopped back on my bed. I knew right away my mind would be buzzing for another hour.

I started out thinking about *Rebecca*, then I moved on to Mrs. Crowe, who was nowhere near as spooky as Rebecca, and then I got to thinking about Brett's scary dad, or whatever he was. Why do guys from the third grade on up like to scare girls? Does it make them feel strong? I don't get it. Scaring people is easy. I could scare anybody. I scare myself sometimes.

Chapter Twenty-six
FROG PEE

Dear Miz Fitz,

I am attracted to boys who do dangerous things. Is that wrong?

— Victoria

Miz Fitz sez:

You are drawn to such boys in hopes that they will return to the cave with a fat, tasty mastodon. Better to have a dangerous boyfriend than to perform such stunts on your own.

LITA

Going without sleep turned out to give me a distinct advantage the next morning: It is best to be fully zombified when dissecting a frog. Not that I was doing much dissecting. I simply feigned consciousness and let Emily do the work since she had the advantage of being tutored by the smartest science nerd in school.

"Not talking much," Emily observed as she peeled back frog skin and popped out something that might have been a liver. Or a stomach.

"Busy being grossed out," I said. "Eww."

"Do anything last night?"

"I read an entire book. *Rebecca*."

"How late were you up?"

"Like, five thirty . . . what are you *doing*?"

"Looking for his pee-pee."

"Frogs have logs?"

"That is what we are here to find out."

"Do we even know it's a boy frog?"

"We do not."

"Maybe we should ask Adam, since he's the expert on all things male and female," I said. "What's that?"

"I think it's his bladder." She poked it with the tip of her scalpel. A thin jet of fluid shot out of the tiny sac and hit me right in the face.

Getting shot with frog piss is not the best way to start off a school day (or any other day) so I did not appreciate Emily laughing and saying, "I guess we found his pee-pee." To make matters worse, I ran to the lavatory and scrubbed my face so hard that I ended up with pink blotches and rub marks. I tried to cover up with my pathetic makeup supply (a minuscule sample jar of foundation), but I only had enough for one side of my face, which was worse than nothing.

Long story short, I ended up on the bed in the nurse's office with a moist towel over my eyes recovering from a frog-piss-induced "migraine." I have never had a migraine in my life but Mrs. Kathryn Fleet, RN, did not know that.

As I lay there, I kept myself entertained by building the perfect imaginary guy. I constructed him from the shoes up, starting with perforated black leather sneakers from Diesel (because shoes are important). I gave him a nice pair of jeans, not the super baggy kind, but the ones where you can tell the guy has two legs. The shirt was difficult. I decided to go with a basic black tee (I could get him something better for Christmas). As for the rest of the guy, the face that kept coming into focus was Brett's. I kept moving his features around trying to make him into somebody else but he kept turning back into Brett. I must have fallen asleep then because the next thing I knew I was dreaming about frogs. Get this: I am dissecting a frog and I touch my scalpel to his little snotwad of a brain, and he says to me, "Kiss me."

I go, "No way. You're a dead frog."

"Kiss me and I'll turn into a handsome prince."

So I kiss him and *poof*! He turns into Adam, only Adam somehow looks exactly like Brett and then the dream gets *really* weird and *that's* all I'm going to say about *that*.

Mrs. Fleet kicked me out just before lunch to make room for a sophomore girl with vertigo. I think the girl was faking but fair's fair. She could have her turn on the bunk watching the ceiling spin (or not). I staggered out into the crowded hallway, made for the lavatory, and checked out my face. Better, but not great. As I was examining myself, the door to one of the stalls opened and Blair Thompson emerged.

I should mention here that I had never exchanged words with Blair. I mean, what was the point? She was her kind of person and I was me.

Anyway, I ignored her.

She went to the next sink over, washed her hands, removed several items from her purse, and went to work on her face. It was hard not to watch. She was very meticulous. Apparently, that slutty, dark-eyed look takes a lot of work.

Naturally, she caught me looking at her.

"Hey," she said.

I nodded.

"You're Lita, right? Adam's friend?"

"I've known him a while," I said. I looked closely at my reflection to avoid looking at her. I was still pretty blotchy.

"What happened?" she asked.

"I got pissed on by a dead frog."

She got it right away. "Frog dissection, huh? I do that next week."

"Watch out for the bladder."

"So . . . you're not Adam's girlfriend?"

"Adam has a girlfriend?"

"I guess that means no."

"*No* is right. Why do you ask?" As if I didn't know.

She looked away. I was pretty sure she was blushing under all that foundation.

"Don't waste your time," I said. "You're not his type."

"What type is that?"

I laughed and shook my head pityingly and walked out of the lavatory into the hall. It was too funny. I could see a guy like Dennis getting fixated on a girl like Blair, but *Adam*? If Blair was interested in Adam she might as well try to lasso a cloud. In the first place, Adam's only true love was his own crazy business schemes. And in the second place, he had way better taste than to fall for a mascara-slathered skank like Blair.

• • •

Later that day I was telling Emily and Daria Trestor about my encounter with Blair. Daria pointed out that last week Blair had worn the exact same outfit to school two days in a row. "That black top with the metal studs, and the black denim skirt with the fake rip up the side. Looked like a castoff from *I Wanna Be a Rock Star.*"

We were laughing about that when Bree Feider slithered up. Emily told her what we were laughing about. Bree listened carefully, no doubt adding the information to her Vicious Gossip Database.

"Some guys really go for the slutty types," she observed, looking pointedly at Daria, who was remembered for losing a pair of highly distinctive panties (black poodles on pink cotton) that later turned up dangling from Stuey Herrell's rearview mirror. Daria claimed they'd fallen out of her gym bag in the parking lot (which was probably true) and that Stuey had picked them up (also probably true). But nobody cared what was true, only what was fun to talk about.

Bree should have known better. Daria took crap from nobody.

"At least I never put my mouth on Hap Ball," she said, naming the largest and most simian of the Wellstone Wailers, our illustrious football team.

I expected Bree to come back at Daria with some snarky comment. Instead, she jerked back as if she had been slapped and her neck turned pink. "That's a lie!" she said, her voice cracking. She turned and stalked off, her shoes clacking on the hard linoleum floor.

"Wow," said Emily. "How did you know?"

"I didn't," Daria said. "I just thought up the most disgusting thing I could imagine. Talk about a lucky shot!"

"Bree and Hap," Emily said with a smile. "You just never know who will hook up."

Chapter Twenty-seven
STRATEGIES

Dear Miz Fitz,

I'm sure you've been asked this before, but is there anything I can do to make my breasts bigger?

— A Cup

Miz Fitz sez:

Eat more food or get pregnant.

ADAM

The faculty parking lot is tucked in behind the school and surrounded by a lilac hedge. I was wedged into the lilacs, waiting, when the teachers started to leave the school at around 3:45. Mr. Hallgren was the first to leave, followed by Mrs. Anderson and several teachers I didn't know. I made a game of trying to match them up with their vehicles. Hallgren had a Buick LeSabre, no surprise there. When Terminator Berman came out, I had her pegged for the H2 Hummer, but she got into a little blue BMW two-seater instead. The Hummer turned out to belong to Mr. Hammer, who coached football.

By the time twenty of the faculty and staff had left, I'd clocked only half a dozen correct guesses. Oh well.

Ms. Ling didn't make her appearance until 4:42, when more than half the parking lot was empty. Carrying a large canvas tote bag over one shoulder and her purse over the other, she walked quickly to a white Toyota Corolla at the far side of the lot.

I emerged from my hiding place and ran up behind her. Just as she was opening her door, I called out.

"Ms. Ling!"

She whirled, eyes wide, tote bag swinging — then she saw who I was and slumped against the side of her car, one hand over her heart.

"Adam! You scared me half to death!"

"Sorry," I said. "I'm not supposed to come back to school till Monday, but I wanted to give you this." I held out my book, all one hundred four pages of it.

LITA

Emily and I were flopped on our backs on her bed with our heads hanging over the edge of the mattress, strategizing. I recommended a five-step program designed to attack all his senses.

"Step one," I said. "Arrange things so you and Dennis are sitting on the same side of the table, nice and cozy, instead of across from each other. So your shoulders touch now and then."

"I like that," Emily said.

"I knew you would. Step two: Cleavage. For visual stimulation."

"I told you — cleavage not available."

"We'll work on that. Step three: Titillate the smell receptors. Wear perfume. Just a little, so he can smell it, but not so much that he passes out. One of those pheromone perfumes. You know, the kind that make male animals want to do it."

"Aren't those illegal?"

"You can get them at Macy's. Step four: Feed him sexy food."

"Like what?"

"Meat. Something like a roast beef sandwich."

"Roast beef is not sexy."

"Not to you and me, maybe. But Dennis is a guy. For some reason they get turned on by roasted animal flesh."

"How about a sausage-and-mushroom pizza?"

"That would work. As for the sense of hearing, you should tell him things he wants to hear. Tell him how smart he is. Tell him he has a great mouth."

"He does."

"Tell him the girls talk about him."

"They do?"

"Isn't that what we're doing? Aren't we girls?"

"I guess."

"Good." I sat up. "Now let's get to work on your boobs."

Emily's breasts were like two smallish grapefruit halves, which was not a bad size for them to be, but there was a lot of space between them.

"It says here to use bronzer to darken the area between," I said, reading from a beauty tips site on the Internet. "Got any bronzer?"

"No." She pulled her T-shirt back down.

"We can use mascara, then. Sort of rub it in to blend it. Then we use some powder or something to lighten the tops."

"Okay, but you have to do it, too."

I hesitated. Not that I was shy, but I wasn't exactly eager to compare. My grapefruits were even smaller than hers.

Emily had lifted her shirt again and was examining herself in the mirror.

"No way," she said, shaking her head.

Ten minutes later our sternums were smeared with mascara and the tops of our breasts were pale with powder.

"That is totally weird-looking," Emily said.

"We have to look at it with clothes on," I said, fastening my bra. "Can you find us a couple of semi-revealing tops?"

Emily rummaged through her closet and came back with a couple of scoop-neck tees.

"Not low enough," I said after putting one on. She went back to mining the closet while I pulled down on the neck of the T-shirt and checked out my newly enhanced cleavage.

Alas, I was not impressed.

Emily produced a salmon-colored taffeta dress with a low neckline. "The bridesmaid dress I wore for Jenny's wedding," she said, pulling it over her head. Jenny was Emily's older sister. The dress was truly hideous — it had an enormous bow over her butt.

But the neckline was perfect. The boobs, however, needed work.

"I think we need to shift them more toward the middle." I pointed toward her closet. "I don't suppose you have a Wonderbra in that rat's nest."

"Nope."

"How about a couple pads?"

One maxi pad under each breast was an improvement.

Two maxi pads was a miracle.

"Oh . . . my . . . God," Emily said, looking at herself in the mirror. "They almost touch!"

"Try it sitting down," I said.

She sat in the swivel chair at her desk and spun slowly around.

"Not bad," I said.

She stopped spinning.

"Cross your arms for me," I said.

Emily crossed her arms.

"Now squeeze."

She squeezed. Her breasts came together and *bulged*.

Chapter Twenty-eight
INFAMOUS

Boys tend to boast more than girls. A guy scores an A on a test and he's running up and down the hall high-fiving and whooping and doing a little end-zone break dance. You don't see girls doing that. Boys need validation. They need it bad.

— **from** *What Boys Want*

ADAM

Funny thing, when I got back to school on Monday morning everything felt different. Yeah, I got a lot of razzing for being the "flyer guy," and I picked up a couple dozen more book orders — I hoped Graves wouldn't find out — but what made it really fun was that I wasn't just Adam Merchant, eleventh grader, I was Adam Merchant, *author.*

I had written an entire book.

"So when do I get my copy?" Bob Glaus wanted to know.

"You didn't order a copy."

"Yeah, but my sister did. And I'm gonna read it."

"I still have to get it printed."

"That sucks."

I saw Lita in the hall after second period. I was a little nervous because last time we'd talked, she'd hung up on me.

"Hey, Leet."

"Hello, Adam." She seemed a little cool. "Congratulations on your book." And a little flat.

"Thanks." I was getting the picture that she wasn't exactly down with me being an author.

"I hope it doesn't have as many typos as your flyer." She turned and walked away.

Ouch! One thing about Lita — when she put her mind to it, she could be a real buzz-kill.

At lunch, I saw Blair for the first time since I'd been suspended. She was sitting alone eating a carton of yogurt. I sat down across from her with a plate full of something that claimed to be turkey tetrazzini.

"Your flyers were a big hit," she said.

"Yeah. Graves loved them. Are you still staying at Hotel Wellstone?"

"That was just for a couple nights. I'm back home now."

"Everything cool there?"

"Everything's fine. You don't have to treat me like I'm an abuse victim."

"I didn't mean that!"

"Not everybody is locked into a traditional family with two parents and one point seven pets and a swimming pool."

"Hey, I don't have a pool. And just one cat."

"I don't need you judging me. Everybody already thinks I'm some kind of a whore. Your girlfriend treats me like I'm a leper —"

"I don't *have* a girlfriend."

"What*ever*. I suppose you told everybody I sleep at school."

"I did not!"

She shrugged. I don't think she believed me. I looked around for something else to talk about.

"Where are Dahlia and Chelsea?" I asked.

Blair flicked her hair back and glared at one of the other tables, where Chelsea was sitting with Bree Feider and some of the other cheerleaders. "Bree decided she needed to include a person of color in her little clique, so she appropriated Chel. I haven't seen Dahlia today. How's your book coming?"

"I finished it."

"That was fast. When do I get my copy?"

"When I get it printed." I was getting tired of telling people that. "Thanks again for helping me the other night."

She shrugged as if she hardly remembered the occasion. "Not a problem."

Just then, Trish Hahn plunked her tray down next to Blair.

"Hey," she said. Trish, with her pale skin, spiky, black dreads, multiple earrings, and the spiderweb tattooed on her arm made Blair look like Little Miss Normal. "Seen Dahlia?"

"Not today," said Blair.

Trish looked at me. "Flyer boy," she said. "When's this famous book going to be out? I got a guy question I need answered."

"What is it?" I asked.

"My boyfriend got a tongue stud, and now he wants me to get one, too, so we can, you know, clank tongues."

"So what's the question?"

"My question is, is he *kidding*?"

I was no expert on body piercing, but I figured I could handle this one.

"Guys like the sound of metal on metal," I said. "I'd say he's totally serious."

LITA

Emily hadn't been able to resist trying out her new look at school. She used the bronzer-and-powder trick and a single maxi pad under each cup (not wanting to overdo it).

She looked amazing.

A couple hours later I saw her, and she didn't look quite so well endowed.

"One pad kept slipping," she explained, "so I took them out."

"Any reaction from Dennis?"

"He asked me how my biology studies were going."

"Patience. Next time we hit him with the whole package."

Adam was back in school and acting like some sort of celebrity. I think what really bugged me is that he sort of *was* a celebrity, even though nobody had even read his "book" yet. I'd heard my mom say that publishing a successful book was fifty percent talent, fifty percent hard work, and one hundred percent marketing. I guess she was right.

I finally got Mrs. Crowe's schedule figured out, so I hit the library right after my last class, when only Miss Morris was on duty. She gave me a couple more du Maurier titles — *Jamaica Inn* and *The House on the Strand* — which I hoped would keep me up nights for the rest of the week.

"I hear we have a famous author in school," she said as she checked out my books.

"If you're talking about Adam Merchant, *infamous* is more like it."

"I'm thinking about ordering a copy of his book for our library."

"Do you really think Adam is capable of writing a book about boys and girls? He barely knows how to have a conversation!" That wasn't true, of course. Adam could talk the ears off a mule.

"I thought Adam was a friend of yours."

"He is," I said. "But this book thing has kind of gone to his head."

Chapter Twenty-nine
ASSUMPTIONS

Nearly all problems between the sexes can be boiled down to one thing: mistaken assumptions. For example, if a guy doesn't get his girlfriend a birthday present, the girl thinks that he is trying to hurt her, when the truth is, he just forgot.

— **from** *What Boys Want*

ADAM

I met with Ms. Ling in her classroom after school. She had my manuscript spread out on her desk. I could see several comments scrawled in the margins. Red ink, and lots of it. I braced myself for the worst.

"Adam, I think your book is very, *very* good . . ." she began.

My heart started to pound. I mean *really* pound, like it was going to rip through my ribs and go bouncing around on the grass. My book was *good*! I tried to say thanks but all I could do was sit there with my mouth hanging open, Dennis style.

". . . extraordinary, really. Especially the question-answer sections.

It feels genuine, it is very clever — I laughed out loud at some parts — and I think it is the kind of book that young people would read."

"It's selling great," I said.

Ms. Ling gave me a sharp look. "You realize that you can't continue to sell it here at school."

"I know, I know," I said.

Ms. Ling held my eyes for a moment longer, then sighed and shook her head. "I wish you hadn't pulled that stunt with the flyers, Adam."

"That maybe was a mistake," I said. "I should have put them on the cars in the parking lot, and paid some other kids to hand them out on the buses."

Ms. Ling laughed. "At least that wouldn't have involved you breaking into the school."

"I didn't *break* in. I just stayed after everybody else left."

Ms. Ling crossed her arms and gave me the *look*.

I said, "So you liked my book?"

"Yes. But you'll need to address a few issues, such as your excessive use of adjectives. You might also want to work on the way the book is organized. Break it into sections, by theme. Right now it jumps all over the place. I've made a few notes here. . . ." She launched into it, tearing my book apart page by page, telling me that I'd made every single mistake a person could possibly make, from misuse of the comma to the order of the chapters. I tried to listen, but after the first two minutes my ears went numb and a dark cloud of despair settled over me.

After a while she stopped talking and looked at me.

"Are you all right?"

"I just finished writing a whole book, and now you're telling me I have to write it all over again?"

166

She laughed. "It's called revision, Adam. Don't look so crestfallen. All you have to do now is make a few changes, get it copyedited —"

"What's that?"

"That's when a copy editor fixes up all the little mistakes — spelling, punctuation, grammatical errors, et cetera — and basically makes the manuscript ready to turn into a book."

"Does that cost money?"

"Adam, everything costs money. But if you are interested in pursuing this, my sister works for Grayweed Press in Minneapolis, and she does freelance editing on the side. I told her you were on a budget. She said she'd do it for a dollar a page."

"You call that cheap?" One hundred and four dollars! I hadn't worked that into my profit and loss projections.

"She also said she could recommend a printer."

I must have looked pretty upset, because she patted me on the shoulder and said, "Publishing a book is incredibly ambitious, Adam. I'm proud of you. Are you going to have a pub party?"

"What's that?"

"A publication party. Invite all your friends and relatives."

I thought about that for a few seconds. "And sell them books?"

LITA

I hadn't talked to Adam since our awkward conversation that morning, but we ended up walking out of the school practically shoulder to shoulder.

"Hey — I forgot to say thanks for the suggestion to read Miz Fitz," he said.

"Did you learn anything?"

"I learned a lot. She's pretty cool."

I almost said thank you, but caught myself at the last instant.

"Miz Fitz knows all," I said instead, then looked away as my eye was caught by a flash of black leather and metal studs. It was Blair, running down the steps toward the curb where a beat-up-looking gray car was waiting.

Guess who was behind the wheel.

Blair pulled open the door and jumped inside. The car pulled away with a deep rumble.

I felt sick.

Adam said, "Who is that?"

"No idea," I said, recovering somewhat. It made complete sense that a grease monkey would hook up with a skank. What I had a harder time believing was that Blair Thompson would be reading *Pride and Prejudice*.

ADAM

The walk home from school was only about twenty minutes, but some days it seemed to drag on for hours. Especially when I couldn't stop thinking about something I didn't want to think about. In this case, Blair Thompson.

It wasn't so much that Blair had a boyfriend — that was none of my business. What bugged me was that we'd spent three hours stuffing lockers and talking about everything, and she'd never once mentioned him.

Maybe he was new — or maybe she just hadn't gotten around to talking about him — but in my experience, girls with boyfriends usually bring it up pretty quick.

I wondered if he had ever spent a night at school with her.

Okay, I admit it — I'd been thinking about Blair a lot. Even when I was working on my book I sometimes would write stuff imagining that Blair would be reading it. It seemed like every time I closed my eyes I saw her face with the flashlight shadows and no makeup.

The thing about makeup is that when a girl uses a lot of it, you see the makeup and not the girl. That's especially true with heavy eye makeup. I suppose if a girl was truly repulsive that could be a good thing, but Blair was far from repulsive, with or without makeup. Before, when I had only seen the made-up version of her, it was like looking at a picture. Then, when I saw her naked face for the first time, it was as if she had stepped out of the picture into reality.

The guy with the GTO must be from her old school. Maybe just a friend.

What was I thinking? What difference did it make to me if she had a boyfriend? I didn't have time to get all twisted over a girl. And even if she was a hundred percent available, I wasn't her type. Not even close. I stopped walking and looked down at the outfit of the day: olive-drab cargo pants, one of my dad's old bowling shirts, and my basketball shoes. Too bad the grunge look was so last millennium.

What had Blair called it? *An undeveloped sense of style.*

Chapter Thirty
THE CLEAVAGE EFFECT

Q: I like this guy but he always hangs out with a bunch of his friends and they do everything together. How can I get him alone?

A: Males travel in packs, because it's the only way to be safe from other packs. Your best bet is to follow the pack day and night, taking care to remain unnoticed, until you see him go off on his own. Then lure him with food.

— **from** *What Boys Want*

ADAM

By Thursday, after working on the book about eight hours every night, I'd made all the changes suggested by Ms. Ling. I'd also made an appointment with Marie, her copy editor sister. I saw Blair in the hall that morning, but we didn't connect — she was talking to Dahlia. I thought I might try talking to her during lunch, but it didn't work out that way.

Dennis, sitting across from me, was eating school pizza and reading *Biology — Life on Earth*. This time he was actually reading it rather than ogling Blair. I guess getting slapped had made an impression.

Blair's little lunch group had grown in size. It was a strange group — they seemed to have little in common other than the fact that they all had wildly different ideas about how to dress. Ardis Lang, for example, was into dark, floor-length cotton dresses that made her look like something out of the 1800s. Melanie and Yvonne Daniels were hardcore goth twins, from their fishnet stockings to their black fingernails. This skinny kid named Raphael something, who nobody much liked because he wore a bow tie and acted as if everything everybody else said was utter drivel, had also attached himself to the group. Blair maintained her usual blasé demeanor, but I had the feeling she enjoyed the company.

However, it's hard to talk to any girl when she's part of a herd. I turned my attention to Dennis. "How's the tutoring going?" I asked.

"Good. I think." He closed his book. "Emily is really smart. I don't know why she thinks she needs a tutor."

"Maybe she just likes your company."

Dennis flexed his brow. "You think?"

"Was she flirting with you last night?"

"Well, I don't know if you'd call it flirting, but she did sit down really close to me. She smelled good."

"How did *you* smell?"

"The usual."

"Too bad."

"Hey, I do not reek."

"Okay, so she's sitting next to you when she doesn't have to. Sounds like flirting to me."

"You know what she told me? She said all the girls in school talk about me. *That* can't be true."

"No, it can't," I said. What I wanted to do was give him a good, hard dope-slap and tell him what an idiot he was, but I've known Dennis a long time. A dope-slap would only confuse him. "The only girl I've ever heard talk about you is Emily."

"Really?"

"Don't you like her?" I asked.

Dennis blinked a few times, and his eyes lost focus. His hand rose up with a hunk of pizza and inserted it into his mouth. He chewed and swallowed, then said, "She has a nice rack."

LITA

"I think it might be working," Emily said.

"Tell," I said. "Tell all." We were sitting on the lawn on the west side of the school doing Coke and Cheetos for lunch.

"He told me I was smart."

"That's *it*?"

"It was the way he said it. He was looking right into my eyes. Like he was trying to see inside me."

"The question is, was he trying to see inside your *top*."

Emily giggled. "He was doing that, too," she said.

Score! "Now all you have to do is get him to ask you out."

"He's kind of shy. Maybe I should ask *him* out."

"I think it's more traditional for you to trick *him* into asking *you* out. That way he feels more manly."

"That sounds like something you might read in Adam's book."

"I haven't *read* Adam's book. I haven't even seen it. Nobody has. As far as I know, it doesn't exist. I can't believe people are giving him money for it." I really needed to change the subject, so I said, "Want to know something tragic? You remember that guy we saw at the bakery?"

"The cute guy with the invisible hat?"

"Him. Guess whose boyfriend he is. Blair Thompson's."

"Wow, I didn't know she *had* a boyfriend."

"I think maybe they hang out at monster truck rallies. Or knock off convenience stores to feed their meth habit." I don't know where that came from. It sounded mean, even for me.

"Blair does meth?"

"I don't know *what* skanky stuff she does. I don't even want to know." I could hardly believe what was coming out of my mouth. Thank god it was just Emily, who would always forgive me for being at my worst.

Chapter Thirty-one
BANKER'S HOURS

Back in the early part of the last century, an actress named Mae West said, "Is that a gun in your pocket? Or are you just glad to see me?" She was referring, of course, to a suspicious bulge in a man's pants. It happens. It swells up and gets, well, hard. Not hard like a rock — more like a zucchini.

— **from** *What Boys Want*

ADAM

I met Marie Ling at her high-rise apartment, a twenty-minute bus ride away. It felt very exotic and strange to be looking out over the city and the river from twenty stories up. I decided that as soon as I made my first million I'd get a high-rise of my own — the whole top floor.

Marie Ling looked like a younger, hipper version of her sister. She had four earrings in each ear, a nostril stud, a pair of retro cat's-eye eyeglasses with tortoiseshell frames, and she wore a pair of baggy, black jeans with about forty pockets. She gave me a Red Bull, popped one open for herself, sat at her kitchenette counter, and began paging quickly through my manuscript.

"For future reference," she said without stopping, "you should leave a one-inch margin. This is actually equivalent to about one hundred twenty pages."

"Does that mean you're going to charge more?" I asked.

Marie continued to flip through the pages, pausing here and there, but never for more than a couple seconds. I got the feeling she went through a lot of Red Bull. After about three minutes she paused, staring at a page. A smile formed on her lips — then she started to laugh. "More like a *zucchini*?" she said, looking at me.

LITA

"Lydia!"

My mother, who had apparently remembered I was alive, was summoning me. I clomped out of my room and down the stairs just in time to see her amputating the leg of a perfectly innocent dead chicken. She pointed at me with the meat cleaver.

"I need you to run to the store for a head of garlic."

"You finished your book," I said. "Congratulations."

"Yes, I — how did you know?"

"You're cooking," I said. "You never cook when you're on the last quarter of a book. And you always celebrate by making chicken cacciatore."

"I didn't realize I was so transparent."

"You're an open book," I said, digging into her purse for money.

There were two grocery stores within walking distance: the Cub Foods over by the high school, and the Byerly's on South Golf Road. I opted for Byerly's. They had great free samples, and it could be most easily reached by taking Holden Avenue.

Masochistically, I couldn't help wanting to see Brett again even if he was a grease-monkey skank-hound. It was like picking a scab to revisit the hurt. Or banging your head against a brick wall to remind yourself you're alive.

But it wasn't all masochism. Now that I knew Brett was unavailable I could fantasize about him without ever having to *do* anything about it.

I strolled up Holden Avenue letting my mind ping-pong back and forth from being ravished by a barbaric lout to seeing that same lout in the company of Skankarella. Of course I kept my head tucked deep in my hoodie as I passed dropout boy's house, sticking to the opposite side of the street.

I did sneak a look, though. Nothing. No legs on the sidewalk. No car. No dirty old man. No Brett. Just the house, blinds drawn, like a dead thing.

"Good," I muttered to myself. But I was feeling a little emptier.

ADAM

I just about died when Marie Ling glommed on to the boner page. But she must have seen me turn stoplight red because she continued flipping through the pages and didn't bring it up again.

I have noticed that older women like to embarrass teenage boys. I don't know why, which explains why I wasn't writing a book called *What Women Want*. I was glad that Marie was editing my book. She seemed nice, and she promised to get it done in a few days and said she'd only charge me a hundred bucks if I threw in two free copies of the book.

The printer she sent me to — The Bindery — was in the basement of a downtown office building. From the stuff on the walls of their waiting room, it looked as if they specialized in printing little books of poetry with stapled bindings and cheap-looking covers. That was okay. I was looking for cheap. The guy who came out to talk to me was a refugee from the 1970s — that's what he looked like, anyway. Lots of hair and a pair of glasses like they haven't made in forty years. And he was old enough to have bought them new. His name was Stan.

"Marie told me you might be stopping by," he said. "You wrote a book, huh? Let's have a look at it."

"I don't have it with me," I said. "I just want to know what it's going to cost."

"Sight unseen? How long is it?"

"One hundred and four pages." I didn't mention the narrow margins.

"Hmmm. Probably about a hundred sixty pages as a bound book. Let's look at some binding options. . . ."

"It has to be inexpensive."

"A man who knows what he wants. Have you thought about a cover design?"

"Yeah. Real simple. Just a white question mark on a black background. As big as you can get it. And the title: *What Boys Want*."

Stan nodded. "Not bad, kid. Could be a bestseller."

"That's the plan." I couldn't help adding, *"Stan."*

On the bus ride home from The Bindery, I went over the numbers Stan had given me. Every business has its ups and downs, I reminded myself. And sometimes a problem turns out to be an opportunity in disguise.

The good news was that Stan said he could fit the job into his schedule next week. I thought that was pretty good. I mean, Lita once told me that when her mother sends in a finished book it takes a year for her publisher to turn it into an actual book. They must be highly inefficient.

The bad news was that Stan wanted $1,538 to print and bind five hundred copies, and I didn't have that much money. I'd have to presell another seventy-five books. That would be tough. The past few days I'd seen orders slack off dramatically. There was a rumor going around that my book was just a scam, and the last couple of days everybody I talked to wanted to see a copy of the book before plunking their money down. I wasn't worried about the rumor in the long term — I would soon have a real book to show, and sales would pick up — but in the short term, the flow of cash had dried up.

That left the Bank of Ted, Ted being Theodore Merchant, aka Dad.

The last time I had negotiated a serious loan from my father was the time I borrowed $149.97 to buy a weed whacker for my short-lived neighborhood lawn-care business. Unfortunately, when I was doing the Hamiltons' yard, I forgot to wear my goggles and got a chunk of something in my eye. The resulting emergency room bill cost the Bank of Ted

$1,200. Even worse, when Mrs. Hamilton backed out of her driveway to rush me to the hospital, she ran over my weed whacker.

The Bank of Ted had forgiven that loan, but my father made it clear that I would have to finance my own ventures in the future. Still, that had been more than two years ago. It was worth trying him again.

When I got home, I was glad to see his car in the driveway. He was usually in a good mood when he didn't have to work late.

It was the best time to beg for favors.

I walked in feeling supremely confident. I would lay out my business plan, show him how it was a win-win deal for all concerned, then tap him for eight hundred bucks. But instead of finding Happy Dad, I walked into what felt like the Jaws of Doom.

My parents, all two of them, were sitting together on the sofa facing the front door, looking somber. Looking at me.

My first thought: Grandma has died.

My second thought: Graves got to them.

They didn't keep me in suspense.

My mother blurted out, "Oh Adam, what ever were you thinking?

"I —"

"He *wasn't* thinking," said my father.

I didn't know what to say, but one thing was sure: The Bank of Ted was closed.

Chapter Thirty-two
THEY MET CUTE

Miz Fitz sez:

Reading is important when choosing a BF. I rate boys' reading ability on a 1 to 10 scale. Example: Reading a STOP sign = 1 point. Entire Harry Potter series = 5 points. *War and Peace* = 10 points. Jane Austen = Marry Me.

LITA

I was coming out of Byerly's, swinging a single garlic bulb in a big, white plastic bag, when I noticed a familiar gray car in the parking lot. I looked around but didn't see Brett. Or Blair. I shifted direction slightly to pass close by the car and sort of casually peeked in through the open window as I went by. No squirming bodies but I saw a couple of paperback books on the passenger seat. *Pride and Prejudice* was gone, replaced by *The Great Gatsby* and *Emma*.

Most strange. I started walking away and was stopped by a voice. "Hey!"

It was Brett coming from the store, carrying his own white plastic bag. His was more heavily loaded.

"Miss Emma Woodhouse," he said, grinning.

Brett was more dressed up than I had seen him before. A nice flannel shirt tucked into clean jeans, and a pair of reasonably greaseless sneakers. Not particularly fashionable, but neat and clean was not a bad start. He didn't even have any smudges on his face.

"Big shopping trip?" he asked, looking at my bag.

"Garlic," I said. "The vampires are coming."

"Looks heavy. You want a lift home?"

"Okay," I said, surprising myself.

Brett got in the car and swept the books onto the floor, making room for me. I gave the seat a once-over, checking for motor oil, or chewing gum, or anything else that might stick to me. It looked safe so I got in. Brett twisted the key, and the engine rumbled to life.

"You like fast cars?" he asked.

"No," I said.

"Okay, I'll drive nice." And he did, starting out smoothly and gliding out onto the street at a sedate pace.

"Where do you live?"

I told him.

"Long walk to the grocery store," he said.

"It's only about a mile."

"All that way for vampire repellent?"

"It's for chicken cacciatore," I said.

"You cook?"

"Not if I can avoid it."

We drove without talking for a few seconds.

"What's your name really?" he asked as we turned onto Holden. "I know it's not really Emma Woodhouse — unless your folks are Jane Austen fanatics who just happen to be named Woodhouse."

"*You* read Jane Austen?"

"For English lit."

"*You* go to school?"

"I just started over at the U."

I tried to absorb this information.

"Turn right on Virginia," I said.

He turned right.

"It's the brown house with the pine tree in front."

He pulled into the driveway.

"Thanks for the ride," I said.

"Not a problem." He smiled, and his eyes sort of crackled. I don't mean a *noise* crackle. It was more of a visual thing.

"My name's Lita," I said.

"Lita what?"

"Lita Wold."

"Nice to meet you, Lita Wold. If I may be so bold . . . how would you feel about giving me your phone number?"

How would I *feel*? Like my lungs were full of soda water.

"What for?" I said.

He shrugged. "In case I need help putting in a new starter?"

"Oh. In that case . . ." I gave him my cell number, then got out of the car.

That was when I happened to notice what was on the backseat.

ADAM

My mom had run into Principal Graves at one of her fund-raisers — she's into lots of causes — and they got to talking.

Guess what they talked about.

"Look at it this way," I said. "I missed a few days at school, but I spent the entire time at the library studying and writing. And I wrote an entire book. That must count for something."

"What you did with your time is not the issue," my father said. "You lied to us."

"I did not. You never asked me if I'd been kicked out of school. I just didn't say anything."

"Mr. Graves told me he sent a letter," my mother said. "I never saw any letter."

"Maybe it got lost in the mail," I said.

My father raised his eyebrows.

"I didn't see any point in bothering you with it," I said.

"Adam . . ." His voice trailed off. He took a deep breath and exchanged a look with my mother. You know the look: *What are we gonna do with this kid?*

I jumped in quickly, before they could announce whatever punishment they had dreamed up while waiting for me.

"Look, I'm sorry. I should have told you. I was wrong. But I was working really, really hard on this book — Ms. Ling, my creative writing teacher, she knows about it. She's read it. In fact, she's working on it with me. And it was no big deal what I did with the flyers — they stuff flyers in our lockers all the time. And I didn't break into the school or wreck anything. Graves wants to ban my book before it even gets printed. And anyway, I apologized and told him I wouldn't do any more book marketing during school, and —"

"Adam!" My dad's voice can be quite loud and sharp when he wants it to be. "Stop talking for a moment and listen. Okay?"

I nodded.

"Principal Graves showed us one of your flyers, and I have to agree with him. That subject matter is not appropriate in a school setting. Are we agreed on that?"

"You should at least read the book before you censor it."

"I'm not censoring anything!"

"Please don't shout, dear," said my mother.

"I'm sorry," said my father. His eyes came back to me. "I'd be happy to read your book."

"Well, you'll have to wait a week. It's at the printer." Lie number one.

"You mean it's being printed right now?" my mother asked.

I nodded. Lie number two.

"Adam! How many copies of this thing did you order?"

"Five hundred." Lie number three, since I hadn't actually placed the order. I felt bad about it, but the lies were necessary. By telling them the book was already at the printer, it was like a done deal. If I told him it was still being edited, they might not let me *get* it to the printer.

"Five hundred! Where did you get the money?"

"I, er, I don't actually have it. Not all of it. Graves sort of wrecked my short-term sales strategy, so I'm short a few hundred dollars. Eight hundred, actually. But that won't be a problem once I get the books — I have a whole stack of preorders."

"But how will you get the books if you can't pay the printer?" my dad asked.

I tried to hide my smile. This was working perfectly. Once I got him talking about the logistics of publishing and selling five hundred books, the whole getting-kicked-out-of-school thing would start to fade.

"I'll just have to come up with it, I guess."

"What do you expect to do? Conjure up that kind of money out of thin air?"

"Actually," I said, "I was hoping I could get it from you."

Chapter Thirty-three
BRASSIERE ANALYSIS

Help me, Miz Fitz!
How do I know if a guy doesn't like me or is just shy?
— ☺*qwertygurl*☹

Miz Fitz sez:

Those two things are not mutually exclusive. Maybe he doesn't like you AND he's shy. Here's a test. Ask him out. If he turns red, he's shy. If he gags, he doesn't like you. If he does both, perform the Heimlich maneuver.

LITA

"You aren't going to believe this," I shouted into my cell phone, holding it with both hands.

"Tell me," Emily commanded.

"The car jockey gave me a ride home from the store."

"Mr. Invisible Hat?"

"That's the one."

"The same car he gave Blair a ride in?"

"Yeah," I said. "But you're *really* not going to believe this: He reads Jane Austen. And he's going to the U. I gave him my number. I mean, he asked me for it."

"You did? What about Blair?"

My mom's voice came crashing up the stairs: "Lydia!"

"I'm on the phone!" I yelled back.

"Set the table! For three!"

"Okay!"

"That was really loud," said Emily.

"Sorry. My dad's on the way home from the airport, and my mom's just finished a novel, so we're celebrating with chicken cacciatore." I took a breath. "As for Blair, I didn't ask him. But she left one of her bras in the backseat."

"How do you know it was hers?"

"It was black."

"Hey! I have a black bra."

"Yeah, but you're no D cup."

Emily sighed. "True."

ADAM

My parents made me promise about six times not to promote, sell, or distribute my book at school. And my loan application was denied.

"You'll have to work it out yourself, Adam," my father said in his no-nonsense voice. "But whatever you do, your responsibilities at school come first."

It was no more than I expected. So when they released me on my own recognizance, I went to my room and called the Bank of Dennis.

Dennis, I knew, had some cash he'd been saving up for a new game system. He also had a considerably larger stash in the bank — a gift from his grandparents for his fifteenth birthday.

"That's for college," he said when I asked him if we could get at it.

"I'll pay you interest," I offered.

"I don't know. . . ."

"You know I'm good for it! I paid you back that fifty bucks you loaned me last year."

"Yeah, but it took you six months to do it."

"It won't be that long. A week or two at most."

"Let me think about it."

I figured I'd better change the subject before he got stubborn and stayed stubborn, so I asked, "How's your love life?"

He didn't say anything.

"Dennis? You there?"

"I was just thinking about Emily. Do you think she's cute?"

"Cute? She looks like the ass end of a rhinoceros."

"What? No way!"

"I'm kidding! Emily's gorgeous. You should ask her out."

"Really?"

LITA

Some people think that simply being a girl is an excuse for being moody, temperamental, unreasonable, and homicidal.

They are correct.

My parents were immersed in their cuddly getting-to-know-each-other-all-over-again mode — doing dishes together, complete with laughter and giggles — which made me feel invisible and made them completely intolerable. I fled to my room and called Emily, which sometimes makes me feel better.

"I called him," she said.

"Who? Dennis?"

"I had a question about cells."

"Cell phones?"

"No. Biological cells. It was all I could think of."

"And?"

"I learned a few things about amoebas."

"Congratulations."

"He almost asked me out."

"You're kidding . . . *almost*?"

"He asked me what I was doing tomorrow night. I told him I wasn't doing anything."

"And?"

"He choked."

"That would be Dennis."

"He said something like, 'How come nobody ever does anything on

Friday night anymore?' Which is, of course, ridiculous because lots of people do things on Friday."

"People who have a life," I said.

"Exactly. Anyway, he started talking about amoebas again, and we never got back to talking about Friday night."

"Boys."

"Exactly. Have you heard from Mr. Greaseboat?"

"No, thank god. The last thing I need right now is a guy with a bra collection in his backseat."

Not that I wouldn't have picked up the phone.

Chapter Thirty-four
BUSINESS

Q: Why don't boys talk?

A: Boys do talk! You watch a group of them from a distance you will see that their lips are moving. They are probably making hand gestures as well. But what are they talking about?

I do my share of talking with my guy friends, but I have no idea what we talk about. Guys have absolutely no short-term memory for conversations. This is why a girl can have a long, heart-to-heart talk with her sweetie, and the next day she makes some reference to what they talked about, and he looks at her with utter incomprehension and says, "Huh?"

The reason for this forgetfulness is that guys almost never say anything in conversation that is worth remembering.

— **from** *What Boys Want*

ADAM

I went straight to Marie Ling's apartment after school on Friday to pick up my manuscript. She was ready for me.

"It looks pretty good, Adam. I made several queries, especially on the last forty pages."

"What's a query?"

"That's where something wasn't completely clear, or when I question some fact or word usage."

"I was planning on taking it straight over to The Bindery."

"Oh, I wouldn't do that! You should take it home, go through the whole manuscript again, and make the corrections on your computer."

I must have looked stricken, because she laughed and patted me on the shoulder.

"Adam, it's a book! You've written it in record time — you shouldn't be surprised that it needs a little tweaking!"

"I suppose. But I thought copyediting was supposed to fix it."

"You're the author. You have to approve all the changes I made."

"I approve!"

She laughed. "Oh, I talked to Joe Wilkins at Wilkins Books. He says he'd be happy to host your publication party. He wants to know when you can do it, how many people you expect, how much the book will cost, and so forth. I told him you'd give him a call."

So I spent the entire weekend revising the book *again*. It felt completely unfair — but she was right. For example, in one place I had typed:

. . . dp,r npud kidy vsmy vp,,imovsyr eoyjpiy s ypp; om yjrot jsmfd . . .

Marie Ling had attached a note saying, "Huh?"

I was going, "huh," too, until I figured out that my fingers had accidentally moved over one key to the right when I was typing, and what I
actually meant to write was:

. . . some boys just can't communicate without a tool in their hands . . .

There were several goofs like that. It took me hours and hours to go
through the manuscript and fix them, and also to figure out all the
"heads" and "subheads" and a bunch of other stuff that Marie said
the printer would need to know.

I did find time to visit Wilkins Books to talk to Joe Wilkins, the
owner. Joe was a small, round man with a few oily strands of gray hair
combed straight over the top of his head, from one ear to the other. He
wore oddly textured, mud-colored pants, and an olive-green corduroy
vest over a brown-on-brown striped shirt. Standing among the crowded,
towering shelves of used books, he was almost invisible.

"Can I help you, young man?" he asked, pale blue eyes blinking
behind thick, greasy, oversize eyeglasses.

When I told him who I was, he said, "Yes, of course. Marie said you
would be stopping by. Who did you say your publisher was?"

"First Man Press," I said.

"Never heard of them."

"This is their first book," I said. I had made up the name that morning. Get it? Adam? First man? "I'm the publisher," I explained.

The corners of his mouth turned down. "Marie did not mention that your book was self-published."

"Is that okay?"

He interlaced his pudgy fingers.

"How many relatives do you have in town?"

"About twenty-five," I said. I realized then what he really wanted to know. "But there are more than twelve hundred kids that go to Wellstone High. I've already sold about eighty books, but that just scratches the surface. If we could get the word out to the rest of them . . ."

By Monday morning, I was ready for the printer. Except for one small detail.

I still needed more money.

The Bindery opened at seven A.M. I was waiting at the door when Stan showed up holding an extra large coffee from Caribou.

"The young author," he mumbled, looking a bit sleepy. He selected a key from an enormous ring and opened the door. "Come on in."

"I just need to drop this off," I said.

Stan looked at the manuscript in my hands as if he had never seen such a thing. "This is your book?"

"Yes." I handed him the memory stick. "Here's the e-version. Marie said you'd need that, too."

"Indeed I do." He set down his coffee and took the manuscript and the stick.

"You said you could print it by Friday," I said.

He nodded. "I'll look it over and give you a call later."

• • •

Since I was forbidden to promote my book during school, and because the manuscript was at the printer and out of my hands, I found myself noticing the other students more than I had been. For example, I noticed that Dennis was looking unusually spiffy. He had on a cotton sweater that looked almost stylish, and a pair of jeans that weren't two inches too short, and his hair was nearly symmetrical. His face looked different, too, but I couldn't put my finger on why.

"Nice sweater, slick," I said.

"I got it from The Gulch," he said.

"What's the occasion?"

"I guess I've been looking a little schlumpy."

"Not that I disagree, but so what?"

He shrugged. "I'm working on my demeanor, too."

"Which means what?"

He pointed at his mouth. I didn't get it.

"I'm keeping it closed." He demonstrated by pressing his lips tight together.

"Nice," I said. "Very grim."

"It was Emily's idea."

"Of course."

"I almost asked her out last night. Only I didn't know what to ask her out to *do*."

"Does it matter? I mean, if she wants to go out with you, you could do anything. Go to a movie, whatever."

"I didn't think of that. Maybe I'll try again today."

"Have you considered my proposal?"

Dennis suddenly looked very uncomfortable.

• • •

I didn't lean on Dennis too hard for the money — I figured I'd save the Bank of Dennis for a last resort. I could tell he was relieved when I backed off.

I saw Blair twice, once at lunch, and in calculus — where Dennis wouldn't look at me because to do so he'd have to look at Blair, too. And Blair was in her attentive student mode, so I spent the entire fifty minutes ignoring Sklansky's drone while I tried to figure out how to let everybody in school know about my pub party on Saturday.

The best way would be to pull my locker-stuffing stunt again, but I was worried about the "profound repercussions" promised by Principal Graves. Then it occurred to me that while Graves had forbidden me to promote my book during school, he hadn't said anything about other people promoting it. If I printed some pub party invitations and gave them to Dennis and Lita and Emily and Bob and Robbie and a few other people — maybe even Blair — they could help get the word out. I'd ask them to distribute them outside of school, of course. And if they did happen to bring a few to school with them, well, *technically*, I'd be in the clear.

LITA

That afternoon I got my period, which explained a thing or two. Like why I'd been so pissed off the past few days. But I'd been pissed off last week, too. And the week before. It was like I had permanent PMS. With Emily being all needy and Dennis besotted and Adam being big-shot-author-guy, I was realizing what a sorry little social circle I was stuck in. I desperately needed some new friends. Or maybe some *old* friends.

The *Wellstone Word* newsroom was a converted utility closet at the end of the darkest, longest hall in the building. Mrs. Hart, the newspaper's faculty advisor, was sitting in a plastic chair in front of a battered desk. Behind the desk sat Sam Johnson. Sam was a senior of course, and proud to a fault of his illustrious position: editor in chief of the school newspaper. *That* would get him into Yale. Right.

The two looked up at me as I stood in the doorway. Mrs. Hart with her handsome, sharp-featured, over-fifty face, and Sam with his pretentious glasses and condescending smirk.

Okay, I told myself, *don't screw this up!*

"Yes, Lita?" asked Mrs. Hart.

"Hi!" I made my voice as perky as I could. "What are you guys working on?"

"Why would *you* care?" Sam asked.

I should explain: Last year, after two months of slaving away on the paper doing scut work like listing club activities, calling local merchants to drum up advertising revenue (ten bucks a column inch, and it was like squeezing blood from a rock), and copyediting the appalling stories turned in by the "senior correspondents" — I had written a sharply worded (and quite brilliant, if I do say so myself) editorial about the declining quality of journalism in today's high schools.

It probably would have been okay if I hadn't plucked all my examples of bad writing from the *Wellstone Word*. In particular, I had singled out the vacuous musings of one Sam Johnson.

Mrs. Hart had killed the article.

So I sneaked it onto the school website.

That was ten months ago. Ten months is a long time to hold a grudge. With the exception of the semiliterate Sam Johnson, I had liked the people who worked on the paper. I'd felt really bad when they all quit speaking to me.

I launched into my rehearsed apology. "Look, I'm really sorry about that thing I wrote last year. I want to apologize. It was unkind and immature and thoughtless. I'm sorry. And I'd like to work on the paper again."

Sam continued to glare at me. Mrs. Hart sat back in her chair and awaited developments.

Sam opened a desk drawer, took out a piece of paper, and read from it. "'Worst of all are those who use their questionable literary skills to advance their own agendas. Case in point, Sam Johnson, whose shoddily written piece on the threatened teachers' strike was a blatant attempt to ingratiate himself with his teachers in order to improve his marginal GPA.'"

"You kept that?" I said.

Sam replaced the paper in the drawer. "'That which does not kill me makes me stronger,'" he said, quoting some dead guy.

"I'm *sorry*," I said.

Sam snorted.

"Now, Sam," said Mrs. Hart.

"That's okay," I said. "I get the picture."

I walked off. Even if I could have talked Mrs. Hart into putting me back on the staff, Sam would have made my life hell.

I didn't need friends that bad.

Chapter Thirty-five
GENDER-SENSITIVE MARKETING

Nothing *trumps food as the key to a boy's heart. Not all foods, however, are suitable for both genders. Boy foods are generally brown in color and high in fat, like triple bacon barbecue cheeseburgers with jalapeño peppers. Other foods are enjoyed mostly by girls, and should never be forced upon a member of the beef jerky sex. These foods include fruit cocktail, yogurt, and salad.*

The only safe food is pizza, which can be ordered with assorted toppings: Triple Meat Lovers Six Cheese Slab Crust for the guys, tofu and lettuce for the girls.

— **from** *What Boys Want*

ADAM

After school, I made up the invitation to the pub party at Wilkins Books. At the last minute, I had an inspiration: I typed FREE PIZZA AND COKE at the bottom of the invitation. There's nothing like free food to bring in a crowd.

Besides, it was my party and I wanted it to be fun.

I ran off a couple hundred copies on my printer, maxing out the ink cartridge, then started making calls. Dennis, relieved that I wasn't asking him for money, agreed to pass out a few invitations.

"Who am I supposed to give them to?" he asked.

"Everybody. Just hand them out."

Emily said she would, too, since Dennis was into it.

Robbie Conseco said he'd do it if Bob did it, but when I phoned Bob he proved to be more difficult.

"What's in it for me?" he asked.

"My undying gratitude."

"Yeah, but I could get in trouble."

"How about a free book?"

"My sister already paid you for one."

"Okay, forget it. Let me talk to your sister."

A few seconds later, Bob's sister, Hanna, was on the phone.

"Hey, Hanna, how would you like to help me with my book project?"

"Sure!" Hanna was a freshman, and impressed by my greater age and maturity. She promised to give invitations to all her friends.

I didn't have much luck with Lita.

"Why should I?" she said.

"Aren't we friends?"

"Yeah, right. Your book was half my idea, anyway!"

"What?" I was shocked.

"We came up with the idea when we were talking. First that time we were watching *Lord of the Rings*, and then later, tubing down the Apple."

"But . . . you said it was a stupid idea. Besides, I'm the one that *wrote* it!"

"Whatever. I'm not passing out leaflets for you." She hung up.

I tried to look up Blair's number, but there were like five pages of Thompsons in the phone book. I'd have to catch her outside the school in the morning.

LITA

I couldn't believe the nerve of Adam asking me to pass out invites to his book party.

Yes, I could. It was typical, self-centered, grasping, totally selfish behavior. Just what I should have expected.

"What's the matter, honey?" my dad asked.

"Why?"

"Because you're sitting on the sofa scowling at the television."

"I always scowl at the television."

"Yes, but usually you turn it on first."

"Adam wrote a book," I said. "It's like I don't even know him anymore."

"Adam Merchant? Wrote a book?" He laughed. "I thought *you* were the writer in your circle. I hear you rattling your keyboard all the time."

"Exactly," I said.

"Jealous?"

Jealous? I gave my dad the most scathing look I could summon up. He laughed nervously and retreated into the kitchen.

Me, Lita Wold, jealous of Adam Merchant? How pathetic would that be?

Fortunately, my cell rang. I snatched it up hoping it was someone who could make me think about something other than myself.

It was.

"Hey," I said.

"Hey yourself," said Brett.

"A brilliant start to our conversation," I said.

"I have to be brilliant? I don't know if I can take the pressure."

"No pressure. Just an observation. Thanks for the ride home the other day."

"You are welcome. So . . ."

"So?"

"So . . ."

For about two seconds, neither of us spoke.

"More brilliant repartee," I said.

He laughed, and I realized he was nervous. "I must be a terrible disappointment to you," he said.

I wanted to ask him about the bra in his backseat, but instead I said, "How are things going at the U?"

"Kind of boring. I'm taking a lot of freshman survey classes, the kind where they teach a bunch of stuff I would have learned in high school if I'd been paying attention. Which of course I wasn't."

We talked for a minute or two about the differences between college and high school and just about the time I was ready to scream, *Why the hell did you call me?* he said, "So . . . do you date older men?"

"How old? Forty? Sixty?"

"I was thinking nineteen."

"Ah. Let me see. I'm checking my rule book. Hmm. It doesn't say."

"I was thinking about Saturday," he said. "You doing anything?"

"Saturday." The day of Adam's party, which I had *not* planned to attend but for some reason — maybe it was the black bra, or maybe I just panicked — I said, "Sorry, I have to go to this book party."

"Oh." I could tell he was trying to figure out whether I really had to go to a book party or was blowing him off.

I wasn't all that sure myself.

Chapter Thirty-six
MANNERISMS

Dear Fitzy,

*My mom wants me to invite this guy I've been seeing over for din-
ner so she can meet him. The problem is he eats like a starving dog.
I'm afraid he will swallow his napkin or something. How can I
change him without hurting his feelings?*

— Sinthia

Miz Fitz sez:

Take him out for pizza before dinner and let him eat the
whole thing. That should slow him down.

ADAM

My invitations-by-proxy went well. At first.

By Wednesday, my agents had distributed all two hundred invitations to the pub party, and I was getting questions from girls I didn't
even know.

"What do you wear to a book party?" asked one senior girl.

"Come naked," I said.

There was a moment when I could tell she was trying to decide whether she should hit me or laugh it off. Luckily, she laughed. "No, really."

"Whatever you want," I told her.

Another girl wanted to know what kind of pizza I'd be serving, and I must have been asked fifty times if coming to the party meant you had to buy a book.

"Not necessarily," I told them, "but you should be willing to consider it."

I never tried to recruit Blair. Every time I saw her she was with Dahlia or Chelsea or somebody, and I was finally figuring out that Blair only treated me like a human being when we were alone together.

On Thursday morning, the hammer fell. The Terminator snagged me right off the bus and marched me into the principal's office. A stack of my invitations was sitting on Graves's desk. Principal Graves was playing with a pencil, doing that waggle thing where the pencil looks like it's made of rubber.

Ms. Berman took up her station by the door and crossed her arms.

Graves continued waggling the pencil until I was seated, then set it carefully on his desk and lifted one of the invitations by its corner, as if he were picking up a dead mouse by its tail. Eyebrows raised, he waited for me to speak.

"You're invited, too," I said.

"Not funny, Merchant." Uh-oh. Calling me by my last name was a bad sign. "I thought I had been clear about this," he said.

"You were extremely clear. I've followed your rules to the letter."

"What about the one about not promoting your book at school?"

"I haven't. I made the invitations at home and gave them to some of my friends. I told them to distribute them outside of school. I guess some of them didn't follow my directions."

Graves and Berman exchanged a look.

I said, "This is really important to me, Mr. Graves. I mean, it's my first book, and Mr. Wilkins agreed to host the publication party at his bookstore. He's the one who told me I should let as many people as possible know about it. And you told me I couldn't even *talk* to people in school about it. What was I supposed to do?"

Graves closed his eyes and pinched the bridge of his nose.

"Merchant . . ."

"I know it was wrong for me to stay after school that day and stuff the lockers, and I'm sorry. But it's not against the rules for me to give invitations to my friends outside of school, and I can't control what they do with them."

"Perhaps. Perhaps not. In any case, it appears that your book party will be a success. That is, assuming your parents allow you to attend — after they hear from me."

"What are you going to tell them?"

"That you are one violation away from expulsion."

"Am I suspended again?"

Ms. Berman cleared her throat, Graves and I both looked at her.

"If he misses any more classes, he'll have to stay after school to do remedial work," she said. "It would result in additional work for our faculty."

Graves gave his pencil one last waggle, then pointed the eraser end at me. "Tempting as it is to deprive myself of your company for the rest of the week, Merchant, I am not suspending you. But I *am* warning you. Do you understand?"

I nodded. He picked up his pencil and rolled it between his hands. It made a clacking sound every time his wedding ring hit it.

"That will be all for now," he said.

The Terminator walked me silently to my first-hour class. As we reached the door, she said, "Good luck with your book party, Adam."

I could have sworn I saw her smile.

At lunch, I told Dennis about my close call.

"No way," he said, dabbing at his lips with his napkin. "The Terminator *smiled*?"

"It might have been a spasm. Did you pass out the rest of those invites?"

"Yeah . . . well, I kind of passed out the last thirty to Mr. Frankel. I mean, he just took them." Dennis cut a small bite of pizza with his plastic knife and fork and put it in his mouth.

"I suppose that's how they got to Graves."

Dennis chewed and swallowed, then said, "Sorry about that."

"It was bound to happen." Then it suddenly hit me that Dennis was eating pizza with a knife and fork, and using a napkin, and not talking with his mouth full.

"How come you're not just cramming it into your mouth like you always do?" I asked.

"I'm working on my table manners," Dennis said. "Emily said I eat like a pig. I'm practicing for our date."

"You asked her out?"

"I did." He grinned proudly. "We're going to your book party."

LITA

"I can't believe you finally got him to ask you out," I said to Emily. We were walking home from school, taking our time.

"Cleavage and food."

"The way to a boy's heart."

"What about you?"

"What *about* me?"

"Are you going to Adam's book party?"

"No," I said. "Yes."

"*That* clarifies things."

"I mean, I wasn't planning to go. But then I told somebody I would meet him there."

Emily widened her eyes and waited for me to continue.

"Brett asked me out," I explained.

"Omigod, you're going out with him? Want to make it a double date?"

"Whoa, slow down." I stopped and grabbed her arm. "There is no date."

"You said no? *Why?*"

"The *bra*?"

"Oh."

"I am not going into competition with Blair Thompson's boobs."

"Why not? I did."

We stared at each other. I was waiting for her to laugh, and she was waiting for me to laugh. Neither of us did. We resumed walking.

"Anyway, I told Brett I couldn't go out on Saturday because I had to go to Adam's book party, and he said maybe he'd show up, too, and maybe we could go out for something to eat after. And I said that would be okay. So I didn't actually say *no*, and I guess I have to go to the party."

"*Have* to?"

"Anyway, I'm going. But it's not a date."

Chapter Thirty-seven
THE BANK OF STAN

The lords of Wanderlust presented the Countess Ravishia with a white stallion, the finest in the land. The countess examined the steed, thanked the lords, then commanded her equerry to dye the beast black.

"Unless you can find a color darker," she added.

— from *Wrathlust Hollow*, **by Carmelita Woldstonecraft**

ADAM

I've had some pretty good moments in my life. Buying my first skateboard, the first time my mom let me drive solo in her car, the time Lita and I found a kitten and my parents let me keep it, and my eleventh birthday when I got my own computer. But the most amazing moment ever was the morning I walked into The Bindery, and Stan handed me a copy of *What Boys Want*, by Adam Merchant.

I took the book in my hands and ran my fingers over the smooth black cover, feeling the heft of it, touching all those hours of work organized and compressed into a rectangular shape that hundreds, maybe thousands, maybe *millions* of people would soon be paying money to read.

Stan stood with his arms crossed, watching me caress the book, a smile cutting across his bearded face.

I flipped through the pages, quickly at first, then more slowly. I stopped at a random page and read a short section:

The male ear screens out things that guys don't want to know — things like how you are feeling, what Jenny said about Brittany, and so forth. But when too many words enter the ear, the brain can overflow and begin to spill words into the brain that most guys are not prepared to handle.

The boy's natural defense against this overflow is to turn off the ears completely and think about something else. Sports, computer games, and comic books are good topics. But for some reason the most common thing is to think about girls other than the girl whose excessive talking triggered the overflow.

It all boils down to this: Too much talking will cause a boy to think about other girls.

It sounded good — almost as if I knew what I was talking about. I must have been channeling Sigmund Freud. Or maybe I'd copied it off somebody's blog — I couldn't remember.

"Nothing I like better than seeing a first-time author holding his book for the first time," Stan said.

"It looks great," I told him.

"Glad you like it." He gestured toward a stack of five boxes on the floor near the door. "You want to take them now?"

"I have to get to school," I said. "Is it okay if I just take a few copies now?"

"Sure."

"Would it be possible for you to deliver the rest of them to Wilkins Books later today? I'm having my publication party there tomorrow."

"I could do that," said Stan. He sorted through some papers on the counter and came up with a bill. "Want to take care of this now?"

This was one of those critical moments. Acting as confident as possible, I said, "I don't have my checkbook. Could you just send me a bill?"

Stan did not react well to that. He held the invoice in front of my face and said, "Which part of COD do you not understand?"

"COD?" I said as if the concept of Cash On Delivery had never occurred to me.

Stan sighed and regarded me wearily. "You don't have the money, do you, kid?"

"Yes, I do!"

Stan cocked a skeptical eyebrow.

"I mean, I have some of it. I'll have the rest after the book party."

Stan's eyes went from me to the boxes full of books and back to me again. I was counting on the fact that he didn't want to get stuck with a bunch of books and no money.

"How much have you got?" he asked.

I pulled out the wad of cash from my pocket and counted it out.

He wasn't exactly ecstatic, but around the time my count passed five hundred dollars, I knew the Bank of Stan was open for business.

LITA

First thing Friday morning Adam came running up behind me in the hall and grabbed my arm and spun me around. He was grinning across his whole face, *way* too much Adam energy for so early in the morning.

I pulled away from him. "Jeez, would you turn it down, Merchant? I can't deal with your ADD this early in the morning." I'd spent too much of the previous night trying to imagine all the different ways my not-date with Brett Andrews might go, and I hadn't gotten much sleep.

Adam was oblivious, of course.

"Check it out! Hot off the presses!" He shoved an enormous question mark in my face.

I slapped it away.

"Adam, cut it out! I have to get to class."

"You have three minutes. Look at it, Leet! Isn't it beautiful?"

I figured out then what he was holding. A book. *His* book.

I took it from him and turned it this way and that. It was very plain-looking: black, with a big white question mark on the front, and the title, and his name. But it was a book. A *book*!

I flipped through it, not really reading, but just trying to absorb the fact that Adam Merchant had written a book. After a few seconds I tried to hand it back to him. He refused to take it.

"I want you to have it," he said. "You were there with me when I thought it up. Besides, we're best friends, right? Even if you are mad at me all the time lately. I wanted you to be the very first person to get a copy."

I was touched, but also kind of pissed. Was he rubbing it in my face? I shoved the book in my backpack and instead of thank you, I said in a completely flat voice, "I have to get to class."

I pushed past him and walked quickly down the hall.

ADAM

Like I said before: Lita was the master of the buzz-kill.

I'd known her through a lot of ups and downs, and I'd gotten pretty good at letting it roll off me, but *jeez!* She could have at least said thank you or tried to fake like she was happy for me. But I wasn't going to let her ruin my big day.

Stan had given me only six copies of the book. The rest he would be delivering to the bookstore. But those six copies were important — I knew who I wanted to give them to.

I caught up with Blair between first and second hour. She was walking with Chelsea. I guess things hadn't worked out for Chelsea with the Bree Feider crowd. I eased up next to Blair and handed her a book.

Blair stopped, staring at the book cover, then looking at me, then back at the book, then at me again.

"Don't let Graves or any of his evil henchmen see it," I said.

"Hey, where's my copy?" said Chelsea.

"You didn't order one."

Wordlessly, Blair tucked the book into her bag.

"Wait a sec," said Chelsea. "I want to see the part about boners."

The third copy went to Ms. Ling.

"Adam," she said, clasping the book to her chest, "I am so proud of you!"

Okay, *that* felt almost as good as seeing the book for the first time that morning.

And what was even cooler was that once everybody had piled into the classroom and taken their seats, Ms. Ling held up her copy of *What Boys Want* and said, "People, we have our first published author!" Then she went on to urge everybody in the class to go to my book party.

It was almost embarrassing. My jaw started to hurt from smiling.

I waited until the end of the day to give away the fourth copy. After the last bell, I went to Ms. Berman's office and peeked through the open doorway.

"Ms. Berman?"

The Terminator looked up from the file she was reading.

"Adam?"

I stepped into her office. "I know I'm not supposed to bring my book into school," I said, "but I wanted you to have a copy." I set the book on her desk.

Ms. Berman regarded the book with her trademark robot stare.

"Is that okay?" I asked.

"I understand you brought another copy to school that you gave to Ms. Ling," she said.

Uh-oh. Busted again.

"But she —"

She cut me off with a wave of her hand. "It's all right, Adam." She picked up the book. "Thank you."

On the way out of school, I was stopped by a few of the kids who had ordered copies of the book, demanding delivery.

"Saturday," I told them. "Come to my book party."

Book number five went to my parents. My dad wasn't home yet, but my mother went all gushy. I was kind of embarrassed thinking about some of the things I'd written about sex and so forth, but I figured what the heck — I was almost an adult, she'd just have to deal with it.

The sixth copy?

That was for me.

LITA

I didn't take Adam's book out of my pack all day because even though I felt bad about being mean to him, I was still mad. Okay, jealous. And it was much more fun to think about Brett Andrews. I spent much of the afternoon putting together the perfect outfit in my head.

When I got home, the kitchen looked as if it had been hit by Hurricane Amanda. My mom was cooking again. She would cook every night until she got started on her next novel. Could be days, could be months. If it was months, I'd probably gain ten pounds. If it was days, we'd be back to takeout and frozen entrées next week.

"What is it tonight?" I asked. "Pheasant under glass? Standing rib roast? Duck a l'orange?"

"Turkey pot pie," she said. "You can't even believe how much work this is."

I dumped my backpack on the kitchen table; the top flopped open and my books skidded out onto the table.

"Don't leave that there," my mom said, gesturing with a boning knife.

"I'll take care of it in a minute," I said. Sometimes it is a good strategy to leave a simple task undone for a few minutes so that they appreciate it more when you get around to doing it. I left the backpack and ran upstairs to check my email.

Nothing but spam. I blogged for a while, answering reader questions in the persona of Miz Fitz.

> *Dear Miz Fitz,*
>
> *I am making dinner for my BF for the first time. What do you think — burgers on the grill, or something fancy?*
> *— Farah Foodie*

> Miz Fitz sez:
> How about turkey pot pie?

That set my stomach to growling so I headed for the kitchen in hopes of scoring a premeal snack. My mother was sitting at the table reading Adam's book.

"Adam really wrote this?" she said.

"I guess."

"It's quite interesting," she said.

"If you like it so much you can have it," I said, opening the refrigerator door. "Do we have anything to eat?"

I looked back at her but the last thing on my mother's mind was what *I* wanted. She was completely absorbed in *What Boys Want*.

Chapter Thirty-eight
MENU ITEMS

Dear Miz Fitz,

When a boy says, "You give me a woody," is that a compliment?
Or just plain rude?

— BopBop

Miz Fitz sez:

I'm going with "rude." Not "just plain rude," but rude with pickles, cheese, and extra sauce.

ADAM

By the time school let out on Friday, at least fifty or sixty people had told me they were coming to what had become "Adam's free pizza party." The problem was that most of them had already ordered a book. In other words, there would be a lot of pizza eaters whose money I had already taken. And spent. That was bad. The pizza was supposed to attract *new* customers. But now that I had promised everybody free pizza, I could hardly refuse to feed the ones who had already bought books.

There was another problem, too. I hadn't given much thought to how I was going to pay for it. I didn't think the pizza guys would be as easy to negotiate with as the Bank of Stan — they would want all their money right away.

"Hey, book guy!" It was Stuey Herrell, who could probably fit two entire pizzas into his long, lanky frame. "What kind of pizza you serving?"

"Anchovy, eggplant, and banana," I said, hoping to scare him off.

Stuey laughed. "Yeah, right."

I spotted Blair coming down the steps toward the sidewalk. She was by herself, so I figured it was safe to approach her.

"Hey," I said. "You coming to my party tomorrow?"

"You already gave me my book," she said.

"Then come for the pizza."

She shrugged and looked away. "I suppose all your friends will be there."

"Well, yeah. It'll be fun."

"Fun for you, maybe."

"I was thinking, maybe after, maybe we could do something. Go grab a bite to eat or something?"

"Who? Me and you and your friend Lita?"

"What does Lita have to do with anything?"

"Never mind," she said. "Anyway, I think I'm busy."

"How about right now? Are you doing anything? Want to go over to Starbucks and cop a cappuccino?"

She looked past me toward the curb. I followed her glance and saw the gray GTO pulling up.

Just then, Brianna Blackmun and Daria Trestor came up and grabbed me, both of them talking at the same time — something about vegetarian pizza — and by the time I turned back to Blair, she was getting into the car.

"— and no olives," Brianna was saying. "I *hate* olives."

LITA

Twenty-four hours in advance is not too soon to start dressing for a party. I had every article of clothing I owned spread across every horizontal surface in my room . . . and I was in trouble. I needed something sexy but chaste, something that made me look great, but that also looked as if I hadn't given it much thought. I flip-flopped from jeans to skirt then back again, from tight to baggy, from somber to colorful, from church choirgirl to back-alley ho. I even, in a moment of insanity, raided my mom's closet. Amazing that after thirty-plus years of buying clothes for herself, my mother had never once acquired an outfit that was not barf-worthy.

Clearly, it was time to call on my higher power.

"Emily!" I said when she answered her phone. "I have a crisis."

"Me, too," she said. "Nothing to wear."

I found my mom in the kitchen cranking out sheets of fresh pasta while an enormous pot of Bolognese sauce bubbled on the stove. I was guessing lasagna. My mother makes the best lasagna this side of the Atlantic.

"Can I use the car for a couple hours?"

"Where are you going?" she asked.

"Shopping."

"For what?"

"Something to wear to Adam's book party tomorrow night."

"Ah, a major literary event! I may have to go myself."

"Please don't," I said. I did *not* want to deal with parental oversight on my not-date.

"Why not?" She saw the expression on my face. "Oh. Sorry, I thought you'd gotten past that being-embarrassed-to-have-parents thing."

"I think I have another year or two to go on that," I said.

Chapter Thirty-nine
PARTY DAY

Dear Miz Fitz,

Whenever I dress real sexy, my boyfriend wants to have, you know, real sex. But when I dress like a slob he just wants to eat or watch sports. What should I do?

— Sexy Slob

Miz Fitz, Rabbit Lover, sez:

There are fashion choices other than "sexy" and "slob." Have you tried dressing up like a giant rabbit?

ADAM

Saturday, an hour before party time, I mentioned the pizza to Joe Wilkins.

"In my store? *Pizza?* Are you out of your mind?"

"I thought it would bring in more business," I said.

"A hoard of teenagers devouring cheese and tomato sauce? They'll spread grease from Alcott to Zola! Impossible! No! Never!" If he hadn't been turning a scary shade of red and spraying me with spittle, it would have been funny.

"I already distributed the flyers and ordered the pizzas," I said.

Wilkins threw up his hands. "Stop! Do not speak another word! There will be no pizza in my store. Not a slice. Not a crust! Not so much as one single anchovy!"

"I ordered ten pepperoni and two veggie," I said, hoping to reassure him on the anchovy issue.

"You are mad! I suppose next you will tell me you ordered a keg of beer and ten racks of extra-saucy spareribs!"

"My dad's bringing a couple cases of Coke."

"No Coke! No pizza! No comestibles of any description! No-no-no-no-*no*!"

I was beginning to think he really meant it. I once saw a guy on TV who claimed that you could negotiate anything. Obviously, he had never met Joe Wilkins. The next thing I knew, he was hauling the boxes full of my books out of his store and dumping them on the sidewalk.

That gave me an idea.

"Hey, Joe," I said as he plunked down the last box. He looked at me, his face flushed with anger and exertion.

"How about if we do it out here?" I said. "Set up a couple tables right here on the sidewalk. Nobody has to go inside your store."

He looked up. "What if it rains?"

There wasn't a cloud in the sky.

LITA

There was no getting my new outfit past my mom without a discussion.

"Lita! Good lord, what on earth are you wearing?"

"Nothing," I said, standing there in my new two-hundred-dollar boots (a *serious* dent in my savings), my new purple skirt, navy-blue leggings, and an ancient denim jacket.

"You are a sight," she said. "I can't remember the last time I saw you wearing a skirt."

"I thought I'd try something new," I said. Emily had talked me into the boots-leggings-skirt combo (tough but sexy). I'd topped it off with my dancing penguin T-shirt (I JUST GOTTA BE ME.) and a faded denim jacket (so no one would think I was trying too hard). I figured I'd hit it from every angle.

"How much did those boots cost?"

"They were on sale," I said. It wasn't true. But they were amazing boots. Almost clunky but with enough of a heel to make them utterly impractical and therefore elegant.

"What's the occasion?"

"Adam's book party," I said.

"Oh — of course!" She grabbed her purse and handed me a twenty-dollar bill. "Will you buy a copy for me?"

"What about the one I gave you?"

"I sent it off to Tess this morning. I thought she'd get a kick out of it."

"Oh. Okay." I took the money and left.

I was half a block from home before it occurred to me to wonder: Who was *Tess*?

ADAM

I was hauling a folding table out onto the sidewalk when a pickup truck blasting hip-hop thumped to a stop at the curb.

"Where's the *pizza*?" Stuey yelled from the driver's seat.

"You're early," I said. I'd been hoping that the first person to show up would be Blair, but instead I had to deal with Stuey, Robbie, and Bob.

"How about you give me a hand with this?" I asked. Robbie hopped out of the truck and grabbed the other end of the table. We unfolded the legs and set it up under the awning. I unloaded a box of books at one end of the table.

Another car had pulled up to the curb. Two girls got out, one blond, one redhead. I recognized them as seniors from Wellstone, but I didn't know their names.

Joe was taping a large sign to the front door:

NO FOOD OR BEVERAGES PERMITTED INSIDE!

"Is this the book party?" the blond girl asked Joe.

"That is correct," he said.

"Are you the author?"

Joe tipped his head toward me. "That is the author over there."

She looked at me and frowned. I guess I didn't measure up to her idea of an author. Her friend was standing at the table flipping through a copy of the book, stopping to read a page now and then.

"Not much of a party," said the blond.

"We're just getting started," I said.

"Let's go, Phoebe," she said to her friend.

"Just a sec." Phoebe — the redhead — was reading intently. Joe Wilkins came out of the store with a cash box and a credit card machine and set himself up at the other end of the table.

The blond suddenly noticed that Stuey was staring at her.

"What are *you* looking at?" she asked.

Stuey rolled his shoulders and made a goofy face — I don't know *what* expression he was going for, but whatever it was, it wasn't what he got.

"Sophomores," said the girl, rolling her eyes.

"I'm a junior," said Stuey.

"I wouldn't brag about it," she said. "Would you come *on*, Pheeb?"

Phoebe pulled out her wallet. "Who do I pay?"

Ka-*ching*!

After that first sale, the flood gates opened. I took my seat behind the table, pen in hand. A couple of girls who had already paid me for books showed up to collect their copies. Joe wasn't too happy about that, but at least he didn't demand a percentage. Marie Ling dropped by with her boyfriend, Chug, a black guy twice her size. While Marie chatted with Joe, Chug stood at the table reading sections of my book and chuckling. He had one of those deep chuckles that hit you in the belly like a sub-woofer. It was good for business. An older woman who just happened to be passing by stopped, took one look at Chug laughing, and bought a book.

"You can sign it to my daughter, Peg," she said.

"Does Peg go to Wellstone High?" I asked.

227

"Peg is forty-three," the woman said. "But she's still trying to figure out boys."

Chug bought a copy, too. He said it was for his little sister.

My parents arrived at seven sharp with a cooler full of soft drinks and another folding table. They had agreed to be in charge of distributing pizza and sodas.

"How's it going?" my dad asked as he set up the table.

"Great," I said. There were about a dozen people milling around, a couple of them looking at the book, the rest of them talking and waiting for the pizza. Another book appeared before me. I looked up and recognized Ms. Berman, the Terminator. Instead of her trademark navy-blue suit, she was dressed in jeans and a maroon U of M hoodie. And she was smiling. I could see her teeth.

"I forgot to have you sign this," she said. "Could you make it out to the Terminator?"

I almost choked. "Seriously?" I wondered how she'd learned of her nickname.

She nodded. I wrote:

To THE "TERMINATOR,"
HASTA LA VISTA, BABY!
ADAM MERCHANT

Ms. Berman *laughed*.

A line had formed, people waiting with books in hand. I recognized most of them from school, but still no Blair. There were a surprising number of kids from other schools. A girl wearing an oversize White Bear Lake letter jacket told me she'd heard about the book party on the radio.

"The guy on KQ was joking about it all afternoon. He kept saying, 'What boys want? Who's this guy kidding? Boys want S-E-X.' Anyway, I thought I'd come down and check it out. I figured you'd be older."

"Sorry to disappoint you."

For the next twenty minutes, I signed books constantly. Then the pizzas arrived. By that time, there were about forty people hanging out in front of the bookstore, and a bunch more inside.

"Hey, Joe," I said.

Joe finished making a credit card sale, then looked at me.

"I was wondering if you could pay the pizza guy," I said.

Joe's eyes, cheeks, and neck bulged, as if his head was about to explode. He reminded me of Principal Graves.

How long does it take three dozen famished teenagers to eat twelve pizzas? About fifteen minutes, or time enough to sign twenty more books. More people were showing up every couple minutes — a lot of them must have heard about it on the radio. Because I was sitting behind the table — usually with someone standing right in front of me — it was hard for me to see. Bree Feider and a couple of her friends walked by, eyeing the crowd to see if there was anyone cool enough to justify stopping. Blair's lunch crowd arrived in Ardis Lang's VW convertible — but without Blair.

I kept looking for her, standing up and scanning the crowd after every couple of books, but saw no sign of her. At one point, I thought I spotted Lita standing back in the fringes, but I immediately lost sight of her behind a cluster of kids I didn't know.

Another customer pushed a book at me. "Who should I make this out to?" I asked.

"*Emily*, you moron," said Emily.

"Oh. Hi, Emily. Hi, Dennis." I checked Emily's name off my list of people who had already paid me, then signed her book, *For Emily, Everything you ever wanted to know about Dennis. Your friend, Adam.*

"Thanks." Emily grabbed her book and melted into the crowd, leaving Dennis behind.

"How's the date going?" I asked.

"Okay, I guess. She seems a little cranky, though."

"Dude!" Stuey Herrell was suddenly in my face, blasting me with pepperoni fumes. "You're out of pizza!"

I looked at Joe, whose eyes went to the line of people waiting to have their books signed. We were both frantically crunching numbers in our heads. Were we selling enough books to justify ordering more pizzas? Joe had griped so much about paying for the first dozen, I was afraid he'd refuse to pay for another order.

A girl came out of the store carrying several books, none of them mine. She walked over to Joe and said, "Can I pay for these here? The guy inside is totally swamped." Joe took the girl's books and started ringing them up. By that time I'd signed three more books, and the line of people waiting for me to sign books had lengthened.

"Order the pizzas," Joe said.

LITA

As soon as I arrived, I realized that I looked like an utter and complete dork. Denim jacket and skirt with leggings? What was I *thinking*? The boots were still fabulous, but after walking almost a mile they didn't *feel* fabulous. I stopped on the outskirts of the melee and looked for someone I knew, hoping for an immediate ride home.

"Hey, Lita." It was Bree Feider. Her eyes raked me up and down. "Nice outfit."

Coming from Bree, "nice outfit" was not a compliment.

"Excuse me," I said, "if you're looking for Hap Ball, I thought I saw him over there." I pointed in a random direction. Bree looked, then blushed. I sidled away feeling worse than ever. Even though I didn't normally care what Bree Feider thought of my clothes, it still got to me. The problem was, I knew she was right.

I scanned the crowd and spotted Emily standing by herself near the bookstore entrance, reading Adam's book. She looked extra hot in her new scoop-neck cotton sweater, jeans, and boots. I would have to kill her for talking me into the purple skirt. I weaved my way through the bodies and came up beside her.

"Hey, Em. How's the big date going?"

She looked up from the book. "Okay, I guess."

Uh-oh. "Okay, I guess" could not be good.

"What's the matter?" I asked.

"Nothing. Dennis went to get me some pizza. He's being really nice and all. I mean, he's being *really* nice. We're going over to Culver's for frozen custard later."

I waited.

"The thing is," Emily continued, "he's like, 'Do you want this? Is this okay? Would you like? Can I do this for you? Are you doing okay?' He hovers around me like a worried mother hen, and it's making me crazy! I sent him off for pizza just to get some space. I think I liked him better when he was ignoring me."

"It's probably just first-date jitters."

"Maybe. Speaking of first dates, when do I get to meet *your* Prince Charming?"

"He might not even show up. And it's not a date. It's a not-date." I scanned the crowd looking for Brett's lanky shape. "Can you believe all the people?"

"You should have been here earlier — Adam signed a book for the Terminator."

"Ms. Berman? No way!"

"Isn't that him? Prince Charming?"

I looked where Emily was pointing. Brett was standing against a lamppost, looking *très* sexy in an unconstructed gray cotton sport coat and jeans. He was smiling and talking to someone I couldn't see. Then the crowd shifted and there was Blair Thompson, laughing, smiling, and flipping her skanky hair back with a skanky, red-nailed hand.

Chapter Forty
FACE TO FACES

Oh, Fitz,

I copied my friend's paper from last year and turned it in. Now I'm scared my teacher will remember it. What should I do?

— Opal

Miz Fitz sez:

Relax. If you're busted, you could tell her that you actually wrote the paper last year for your friend, and it is your friend who should have been busted. Not a nice thing to do to your friend — I'm just giving you your options.

ADAM

By the time the second wave of pizzas arrived, I had sold a ton of books, and the crowd was spilling from the sidewalk onto the street. Bree Feider and her friends returned — apparently, the party had gotten big enough to merit their attention. I sold books to three of my ex-girlfriends: Tracy Spink, Bridget Murphy, and Ashley Strickland. Even Miss Morris bought a copy for the school library.

Sam Johnson, the editor of the *Wellstone Word*, asked if he could interview me. I was trying to answer his questions and sign books and remember people's names — all at the same time — when I saw Blair. She wasn't alone. Standing next to her, talking and laughing, was the guy with the GTO.

LITA

I had three choices. I could walk right up to Brett with a big smile and try to out-sexy Blair, which would be tough. Or I could slink away like a whipped dog.

Or I could simply die.

I chose number three, beaming a death wish skyward. I waited for a count of ten. Where was that bolt of lightning when I needed it?

Okay, dying was out. Slinking away was not an option, either. Lita Wold lurks, spies, lies, sulks, cries, and mopes, but she does not *slink*. I looked down at my carefully chosen dork rags and sighed.

Whenever my father was entering into some questionable venture (like trying to fix a leaky faucet), he would roll up his sleeves and say, "In for a dime, in for a dollar."

"That's stupid," I would say back to him.

He would laugh, then go right ahead and do whatever it was he was doing, until either he fixed it or my mom called the plumber.

But now it made sense to me. I'd bought the boots and the skirt. I was committed to my program of social suicide. Never mind that Blair's outfit (sprayed-on black leather jeans, and a scoop-neck top revealing more cleavage than Emily could ever hope for) made my getup look like a nun's habit.

At least my boots were way cooler than hers.

I circled around the crowd so I could come up behind them. I don't know why. Yes, I do. I didn't want Blair to see me coming. I was afraid if I had to walk right into her stare, I'd choke or trip over my own feet.

Once I got my angle right, I took dead aim and marched toward them. As I got close enough to overhear their conversation, I slowed down.

"What kind of high school kid writes a book?" Brett asked.

"Adam is sort of different," Blair said.

I felt a little twinge of pride hearing her say that. I was about to accidentally bump Brett's shoulder when Blair said to him, "So what are *you* doing here?"

That was a surprise. I assumed they had come together.

Brett gave a faint one-shoulder shrug and said, "I'm meeting somebody." He scanned the crowd, but didn't look in my direction. "I feel like I'm back in high school. Everybody seems so young."

"Young like me?" Blair said.

"Yeah, but you're wise beyond your years."

They both laughed, and it hit me hard how *comfortable* the two of them seemed together. I was standing maybe four feet away from them, and they were totally oblivious in their own little world while I was this high schooler wearing stupid clothes and mooning over a college boy. I had to leave. I spun around and caught the sharp edge of the new heel on my new boot (the left one) in a crack. A yelp leapt from my mouth and I went down, landing hard on my butt, my booted feet flying higher than my head. This was my exact position when Brett and Blair turned to see what all the yelling was about.

ADAM

"Where did you get the idea for your book?" Sam Johnson asked.

"I . . . er . . . huh?" I was trying to keep an eye on the GTO guy, but people kept getting in the way, and Sam kept asking me questions. Another person shoved a book in front of me. Chelsea Whalenburg.

"I decided to buy your book," she said, "even though I already *know* what you all want."

"And what is that?" Sam asked her.

"My *ass*," said Chelsea.

Sam smiled and scrawled something in his notebook. I signed Chelsea's book.

"You were saying?" Sam asked after she left.

"I got the idea one day when I was tubing down the Apple River with some friends, and we were talking about how guys are always trying to figure out girls and vice versa, and I —" My mouth stopped talking. There he was, the GTO guy, only it wasn't just Blair standing next to him — Lita was there, too. And then Lita got knocked down or something, and all these people were gathering around, looking down at her.

Chapter Forty-one
MINOR VIOLENCE

Dear Miz Fitz,

My boyfriend is superhot so a lot of girls think up reasons to talk to him. It drives me . . .

. . . Out of My Mind

Miz Fitz sez:

Maybe he is too hot for you. Send me his photo, name, and phone number. I will check him out and get back to you.

LITA

What was there to say?

I said, "Ouch."

Brett grabbed my hand and helped me to my feet. My rear end was in shock, but at the moment the only bruising that concerned me was that of my ego.

Blair, checking out my footwear, said, "Nice boots."

Brett looked from me to Blair and back again.

"You guys know each other?"

"Not really," we both said at once.

"I was looking for you," Brett said.

Blair's eyes went big. She slapped her hand over her mouth, turned, and walked away. I enjoyed a nanosecond of triumph, followed by a sinking feeling as in, *Wait . . . was she* laughing *at me?*

Maybe Brett was one of those guys with a dozen girlfriends. Maybe Blair was laughing (*Had* she been laughing? I couldn't decide. . . .) because she knew I was next in line for mortification and heartbreak. Or maybe because she *knew* I didn't have a chance with him because there was no way I could compete with their history. Or with her skanky boobs.

"— looks like your friend is getting his fifteen minutes of fame," Brett was saying.

I looked over at Adam. He was talking to Sam Johnson.

"You sure you're okay?" Brett asked.

"I bonked my butt, not my skull," I said.

Brett grinned, which pretty much erased every thought in my head for the moment.

"Come on, let's see what the famous author is saying." He grabbed my hand and pulled me through the crowd.

ADAM

"How long did it take you to write it?" Sam asked.

"About a month," I said, trying to keep an eye on Lita, Blair, and the GTO guy. People kept getting in the way, but I could see that Lita was back on her feet and seemed to be okay.

"Would you be willing to read a section?"

"Right now?" Blair was walking away from Lita and the guy.

"Yeah. I'd like to post it on the online version of the *Wellstone Word*." Sam took a camcorder from his shoulder bag. "I'll set this up here." He grinned. "Why don't you read the part about boners?"

"Um . . . maybe I should read something else."

"Suit yourself."

Several people noticed the camera and started to gather around as I flipped through a copy of my book, looking for a short section to read. I wanted something slightly provocative, but not totally embarrassing. I found what I was looking for under the chapter titled "Body Parts."

I cleared my throat and looked into the lens.

"Okay?" I asked.

"Go ahead," said Sam, pressing a button.

I began to read: "'Question: Why are boys obsessed with breasts? Answer: They aren't. Boys are obsessed with themselves. Breasts are several notches down the list — after cars, games, and food. However, it is true that boobs can grab a guy's eyes like nothing else in the known universe.'"

Sam nodded, telling me to keep going.

"'It's not just boys who can't help gawking — girls do it, too. But boobs are not the bottom line when it comes to sexual attractiveness. Most guys prefer girls whose knockers cannot be deployed as deadly weapons. Nevertheless, there is no eye magnet more powerful than an ostentatiously displayed bosom. Therefore, girls think guys want nothing more than a girl with a rack. They are wrong. Guys want to LOOK at boobs. They like looking at monster trucks, too. That doesn't mean they want one in their driveway.'"

Several people laughed at that. I looked up and saw Blair smiling at me. Dennis and Emily were listening, too.

Then I noticed Lita and the GTO guy. Something was wrong. Lita was staring at me with an expression I had never seen before. Shock? Pain? Anger? It was all there.

I forced myself to keep on reading.

"'It's like girls looking at shoes. You maybe can't take your eyes off those eight-hundred-dollar thigh-high red calfskin boots, and you might even fantasize about wearing them, but that doesn't mean you will.'"

I closed the book.

"Good job," said Sam, lowering the camera.

"I gotta take a break," I said. I stood up, scanning the crowd for Lita, and found her standing near the empty pizza boxes, her back to me, furiously paging through a copy of my book. I walked over to her.

"Leet? You okay?"

She snapped her head around, followed by her arm. I saw the book coming at my face, but it was too late to duck. The spine hit the bridge of my nose edge-on; the world flashed red. I staggered back, tripped, and fell onto the book table. The table collapsed, sending the books, the cash box, and Joe Wilkins onto the sidewalk.

I climbed to my feet, half-dazed, blood spilling from my nose onto my shirt. Lita was right there in front of me.

"You *asshole*!" she shouted in my face. I tried to back away, but stepped on a pile of books and fell down again. "You are a thief, Adam

Merchant, and you're not getting away with it!" Someone grabbed her by the arm — the GTO guy.

"Getting away with what?" I asked, holding my hand over my nose.

She tried to come at me again, but the GTO guy held her back.

"Let GO of me!" she shouted, kicking his shin with her heel. He let go and hopped backward on one foot, straight into Blair, knocking her to the ground.

Lita kicked at the books scattered on the sidewalk. "I knew you couldn't write a book like this yourself. Plagiarist!" She scooped up an armful of books and dumped them on me. "Did you write *any* of this? Or did you steal it *all*?"

I was scared. Lita stood over me like a mad avenger, white-faced, hard-jawed, and quivering mad like I'd never seen her before. Her nostrils were flared and her hands were knotted into sharp, bony fists. I outweighed her by about eighty pounds, but in that moment I knew she could seriously hurt me.

I said, "I wrote it! I took some stuff off the web, sure — but I *changed* it! Besides, it was just from blogs and stuff."

She laughed, a tight, high-pitched sound. "You are pathetic."

Then she turned her back and ran.

Chapter Forty-two
MOSTLY ORIGINAL

Guys have four personalities: the one they use with their parents, the one they use around other adults, the one they use for talking to girls, and the one they use for hanging with their friends. Leakage between the various personality types can cause serious problems.

— from *What Boys Want*

LITA

I lasted about two blocks before my feet told my brain that they were about to disintegrate. I slowed to a hobble, then stopped completely and just stood there on the sidewalk like a cyborg whose programming had expired. I must have been standing there three or four minutes when I heard a car pull up beside me.

It was Brett. I turned my back, too embarrassed to face him.

"Remind me to never get on your bad side," he said. I heard him open the car door. "If I touch you, are you going to hurt me?"

"I can't promise anything," I said. A moment later, I felt his hands on my shoulders. I let him turn me around and hug me, my own arms dangling uselessly at my sides. I wondered how many times he'd hugged Blair like this, but I was afraid if I asked he'd stop. After about twenty seconds, he unhugged me and held me by my shoulders at arm's length and looked into my face.

"Are you all right?" he asked.

"I'm fine."

"You going to tell me what that was all about?"

"Not right now."

"You were pretty scary," he said.

"Can you give me a ride home?" I *really* did not want to talk about it.

"Sure. Unless you'd rather go get something to eat? Or go to the gym and punch out a speed bag?"

"Not funny."

We got in the car and rode in silence for several blocks. I sat with my jaw clamped shut, staring out the windshield.

"You're a fascinating person, Lita Wold," he said.

That got my attention. If he had told me I was beautiful or if he had told me he loved me or if he had said he understood me, or any of a hundred other common lines that guys use, I would not have believed him. But *fascinating*? How could I argue with *fascinating*?

"Why?" I asked. "Because I'm violent and insane?"

"Well, there's that. But I was thinking more along the lines of passionate and intense."

"I get mad sometimes," I said. "Don't you?"

"Never." He looked at me and smiled — you know the way a guy smiles when he really likes what he's seeing? "You look like a little kid all slumped down like that with your arms crossed."

"Maybe I am a little kid. You could be arrested for taking advantage of a minor."

"Are you hungry, jailbait?"

"Not really." I thought for a moment. "But I could go for a milk shake."

ADAM

It was starting to get dark by the time I got my nosebleed stopped and cleaned up my face. Outside the bookstore, most of the crowd had left. I didn't see Blair anywhere. Dennis and Emily were hanging out near Dennis's mom's minivan. Joe was behind the table packing books back into their boxes, my mom and dad were stacking empty pizza boxes and picking up empty soda cans, and Sam Johnson was waiting in ambush just outside the door.

"Adam!" he said, aiming his camcorder at me.

"Sam, can we do this later?" I said.

"Just one question — is it true that your book is plagiarized?"

I stared back at him, trying to think how I should reply. I'd copied some of the book off the web, sure — but I had *changed* it. The words weren't exactly the same. Wasn't that all right? And besides, weren't websites what they call public domain? And even if I had copied some of it, what had gotten Lita so cranked?

"I wrote the book," I said. "Now get that camera out of my face." I walked over to Joe. "How many books did we sell?"

"Eighty-nine," he said, "not counting the ones you'd already been paid for."

"Did I hear you say eighty-nine?" asked Sam.

"That's right," said Joe.

Sam made a note, then took out his wallet. "Better make it ninety," he said. "I'm going to run a review in the paper. And I might want to do a follow-up interview — depending on what I find on the web."

I signed a book for him, but I did not like the way he was smiling at me.

It didn't take long to clean up and haul the tables back into the store. Joe figured out the exact sales, deducted his percentage and the cost of the pizzas, then wrote me a check for $770.40.

"You'll be taking the rest of these books with you, I presume," he said.

"Don't you want some for the store?" I said.

He looked at me, very serious. "Not unless you can clear up these allegations of plagiarism," he said.

"I can clear it up right now. I wrote this book."

"Then why was that young lady so upset?"

"I have no idea."

"I heard you say you'd copied some of it off the Internet."

"Yes, but I *changed* it. The actual words are mostly original."

"Mostly?"

"Almost entirely."

Joe shook his head.

...

We loaded the unsold books into my parents' car. "Are you coming home with us?" my mother asked.

"I think I'll walk," I said. I reached up to touch the bridge of my nose. It was sore and lumpy. I'd never thought of books as deadly weapons before. I supposed they would soon be outlawed on international flights. Lita would think that was funny. I fought back a nasty, queasy feeling in my stomach. Had I really copied that much? I tried to remember those long hours of cutting and pasting and changing sentences around. Were blogs copyrighted? Had I made enough changes to make it okay? I thought I had. But I wasn't sure. And how had Lita even noticed?

I wondered what Sam Johnson would find when he started googling lines from my book. It made me feel like throwing up. Needing reassurance, I put my hand in my pocket and felt the stiff, thin paper of the folded check. I took it out and looked at it again.

Seven hundred seventy dollars and forty cents.

Almost exactly what I owed Stan the printer.

My parents drove off, leaving only me and Dennis and Emily standing in front of the bookstore. They looked as lost as I felt.

"I thought you two were going out for ice cream or something," I said.

"We're thinking of going for a burger," Dennis said. "You want to come?"

"No, thanks," I said. The burger part sounded good, but I had no desire to be the third wheel on their first date.

"Are you *sure*?" Emily said with a whine in her voice. "It would be *fun*."

"I don't think so," I said. What was going on with these two? Emily was giving me this pleading look, like she was desperate for me to come along. Wasn't she supposed to have this huge crush on Dennis? Why would she want *my* company?

Dennis said, "So what was all that with Lita?"

"I guess she got mad about something," I said. The understatement of the century.

"Is it true what she said?" Dennis asked. "About you copying the book?"

"I just borrowed some stuff off a couple blogs and changed it around some. No big deal."

Emily was flipping through her copy of the book.

Looking past her, I saw a familiar figure step out of a Caribou Coffee half a block down the street. Blair.

Emily said, "Some of this does look pretty familiar. . . ."

"Gotta go," I said, and I ran.

Chapter Forty-three
THROWBACKS

Q: What makes boys and girls so different?

A: Boys and girls are not all that different. We all eat, sleep, love, cover ourselves with fabrics, feel pleasure and pain . . . the list is nearly endless. The differences we think are important — variations in communication technique, reproductive equipment, and taste in movies — are relatively minor. But those minor differences are, subjectively, major.

— **from** *What Boys Want*

ADAM

"Blair!"

She turned and waited for me to catch up. I noticed she was carrying a copy of my book.

"Party's over?" She looked at my face. "Ouch. She nailed you good."

"More embarrassing than painful. But, yeah, it hurts."

We started walking, shoulder to shoulder.

"You hungry?" I asked.

"I read someplace that food is the way to a boy's heart."

"You read my book already?"

"Some of it."

"Learn anything?"

"Yeah. More than I ever wanted to know about erections."

"When my parents read that part, they'll probably have me castrated."

"Unless your friend Lita does it first. What made her so mad?"

"I guess she thinks I copied everything in my book. Lita can get pretty torqued."

"I'd say so."

We walked for a while without talking.

"Aren't you going to ask me if I copied it?" I said.

"Nope."

"I didn't copy most of it."

Blair didn't say anything.

"I mean, I copied some of it, but I changed the words around so, you know, it would be okay. I don't think I broke any laws or anything."

"I get it," she said. We didn't talk for about twenty paces, then she said, "I knew this girl who used to write papers for other kids at the school I used to go to. She was really good at it. She used to charge, like, thirty bucks for a guaranteed A. It got to where she was writing ten or fifteen papers a month. Like for the entire football team."

She stopped talking. A few seconds later she started up again.

"The money was really good, but it was a lot of work, so she started doing what you were doing — copying stuff off websites and then changing the words around. Like she'd change 'During the Great Depression of the 1930s, Roosevelt created the New Deal' to 'Roosevelt created the New Deal during the Depression of the 1930s.' The same, but different enough so that if a teacher googled a sentence, he or she wouldn't find anything.

"At first it worked great because there's so much good stuff on the web. She made sure every paper was different. But after a while some of the teachers started noticing that some of their most dim-witted students were turning in this A work that all sounded kind of the same. Long story short, she got busted big-time. And pretty much all of her friends were like, 'We don't know you, bitch' — because she'd done papers for them, too, and they were afraid they'd get busted just for hanging with her. So she basically said screw you to everybody including her teachers, and they kicked her out of school."

"Then what happened?" I asked after a few seconds.

"Then I moved here. It was a long time ago. So where do you want to eat?"

On foot, our choices were limited. I ran down the list: "Dairy Queen, The Wagoneer, Beek's Pizza . . ."

"No pizza," she said. "Watching all those pizzas being gobbled grossed me out. Something hot would be good, though." Bumping shoulders with me. "I'm kinda cold."

Without giving myself time to think about it, I put my arm around her shoulder. It was the right move — she leaned into me. I shortened my steps to match hers, but at the same time she lengthened her stride, and we nearly fell. Blair laughed.

"How about The Wagoneer," I said. "Good fries."

"Sold," she said as our feet found a rhythm together.

LITA

"You've never been to The Wagoneer?" I asked Brett.

"I've only been living on this side of town for six months," he said.

"You'll fit right in — all the seventies throwbacks hang out there."

"Thanks a lot!"

"The food's pretty good, too," I said. I gave him directions. So far, he hadn't asked me any more questions about why I'd gone insane at the book signing. I appreciated that. I wasn't ready to out myself as Miz Fitz. At least not until I could get to a computer and delete some of my more incriminating posts. Or maybe just shut it down altogether. But if I shut it down, I wouldn't be able to prove to everybody that Adam had copied half his book from my blog. I kept going back and forth trying to figure out what to do and getting madder and madder at Adam every second.

"Hey," Brett said. "You okay?"

I snapped at him. "I wish you'd quit asking me that!"

"Whoa, what did I say?"

I took a breath. "Nothing. Sorry. I was thinking about something else."

"Can I ask you something?"

"Take a chance," I said.

"How come you're mad all the time?"

"Because life sucks and then you die?"

"Seriously."

"Sorry," I said. "That information is classified." Which was true. It was so classified that even I didn't know the answer.

The Wagoneer was a brick-red wooden shack not much larger than a two-car garage, surrounded by a large, corrugated canopy supported by white posts. About a dozen cars were parked beneath the canopy.

"See?" I said, pointing at one of the cars.

"Seventy-two Cutlass," Brett said. "Nice."

"Like I said, Throwback City."

Brett pulled into a spot between the Cutlass and an SUV. People were sitting in both vehicles, eating.

"How do we order?" Brett asked.

"Roll down your window and wait."

According to my parents, there used to be a lot of drive-in restaurants where a waitress would come out to your car, hand you a menu, take your order, then bring you the food on a special tray that hooked over the driver's side window. People would eat in their cars and when they had finished, the waitress would come to take the tray away. Going to the drive-in was a social event. Or so I've been told.

But all that was in the days before the invention of the drive-thru window. Now you go to McDonald's or KFC or whatever and they hand you your food in a bag and you take it home or eat it while you're driving. Nearly all the old-time drive-ins are history. Except for a few like The Wagoneer, which got caught in a time warp.

I could see the waitress coming. Brianna Blackmun.

"Need menus?" she asked Brett.

I leaned forward so she could see me. "Hey, Brianna."

"Lita! Hi. Did you go to Adam's book thing?"

Brett started to say something, but I dug my knuckle into his arm and whatever he'd been about to say turned into "Ow!"

"Yeah, we went," I said. "You didn't miss much."

"I'll give you guys a minute," Brianna said, handing us a couple of menus. "I got to check on — oh, hey, did you know Emily's here with Dennis?" She pointed at a minivan a few spaces over, then went to take an order from another customer.

"How come you're always hitting people?" Brett asked, rubbing his arm.

"I'm not," I said.

"You hit your friend with a book, you kicked me in the shin, and you just gave me a knuckle punch."

"Sorry. I'm having a bad night. I'm not usually this psycho bitch."

"Glad to hear it."

"Just lately I've been getting mad a lot. But I promise not to hit, kick, or claw you for the rest of the night."

"What about tomorrow?"

What was *that*? Did that mean he wanted to see me *again*?

"Okay, I promise never to hit, kick, or claw you unless you do something really rotten."

"Why do I not find that reassuring?" Brett smiled, taking the sting out of it. "Who are Dennis and Emily?"

"Just some friends. They were at the party." I shouldered open the door. "I'm going over to say hi."

Chapter Forty-four
THE TWO BLAIRS

Q: I talk about my boyfriend all the time when he is not around.
Does he talk about me?

A: No. But that doesn't mean he's not thinking about you.

— **from** *What Boys Want*

ADAM

There were two Blairs.

Blair Number One was the one everybody — including me — saw most of the time. Blasé, distant, sarcastic, hiding behind her makeup, disdainful of lesser creatures, impossible to get close to. That Blair — the public Blair — was in control whenever there were more than two people present.

Blair Number Two — the one I had met for the first time the night we stuffed the lockers, and the one sitting across from me at The Wagoneer — was an entirely different creature. She smiled. She looked *at* me instead of *through* me. And she was fun to talk to. *That* Blair showed her face only when we were alone.

Sitting at one of the picnic tables under the corrugated fiberglass awning, we sipped cherry Cokes and talked as we waited for our food to arrive. Most Wagoneer customers eat in their cars, but there are a few picnic tables for people who don't want to get food all over their upholstery, or for people like us who show up on foot.

A pair of heat lamps cast a reddish glow across the table. The cool air was steamy with the aroma of fried food. Our conversation jumped all over the place, from laughing about Dennis and Emily — Blair thought they were a cute couple — to lunchroom politics. Blair thought it was hilarious how she and all the fashion misfits — Trish, Dahlia, Ardis, Raphael, and the goth twins — had found each other. We also discussed the finer points of hamburger preparation. She liked her catsup *under* the meat, ". . . so the red tanginess hits my tongue first."

I wanted to ask her about the GTO guy, but I was afraid of what she'd say. When you're having a great time with somebody, the last thing you want to do is say something that will screw it up. I told her my theory about Blair One and Blair Two, which was only mildly risky, or so I hoped.

"When we're in school or around other people, you act kind of like you're too cool to talk to me. But when we're alone, you're really nice."

"Oh." She looked at me hard and long, as if she was trying to figure out how much she could trust me. She said, "Don't *you* act different in different places? Like, I bet you act different around your parents than around your friends."

"True."

"People in groups are like sheep. Like, when your very best friend is surrounded by other people, she cares more about what everybody else thinks than she cares about you. The more people there are, the more they act like animals."

"That doesn't make sense."

"Sure it does. Have you ever heard of two guys getting in a fistfight when there's nobody around to watch? It never happens. It takes a crowd to bring out the beast. You can't trust anybody when you're not alone with them. Anybody. You have to have boundaries."

"I'm the same person at school as I am now," I said.

"No, you're not. And neither am I."

"You mean I can't trust who you are except when we're alone together?"

"Not as much."

"Like when you're with that guy?" There. I'd said it.

"What guy?"

"The guy with the GTO."

"Oh. My. God." She rolled her eyes toward heaven. "Are you talking about *Brett*?"

"That's his name? Brett?"

At that moment we were interrupted by Brianna Blackmun with our tray of food.

"It is so busy," Brianna said as she put our burger baskets on the table. "*Everybody's* here tonight. I even saw Dennis and Emily on, like, a *date*."

"There he is now," said Blair, pointing toward the order window. Dennis was waiting outside the service window, looking anxious.

"He's waiting for them to scrape the mayo off Emily's veggie burger," Brianna said.

LITA

Emily was sitting by herself in the minivan, window down, slumped against the door.

"Hey, Lita," she said listlessly.

"I thought you guys were going to Culver's," I said.

"We did, but it was, like, crazy busy. The entire Wellstone football team was there. Dennis got all anxious so we decided to come here. He treats me like I'm gonna break if somebody looks at me wrong."

"Where is he?"

"Over at the window. When our food came, I said, 'Oh, I forgot to tell her no mayo.' He grabbed my food and took it back. Like a little mayo is going to kill me. He's driving me nuts. And he smells weird."

"Weird how?"

"Flop sweat."

"He'll get past that. Give him time."

"I don't know. . . ."

"You're not in love anymore?"

"I just wish he'd calm down. Are you here by yourself?"

"I came with Brett. We —"

I was interrupted by Dennis, who came running up with Emily's burger basket, saying, "Mayo crisis averted! I just saw . . . hey, Lita! Guess who I just saw."

ADAM

Blair was right — it was definitely tangier with the catsup *under* the meat. In fact, it tasted so good I actually took about five minutes to devour my burger and fries. I did it by savoring each bite, then counting to ten between each chomp.

I was down to my last few fries when Dennis finally got the mayo-free burger he'd been waiting for. He started back toward his car, but must have seen me and Blair out of the corner of his eye because he twisted his head back toward us before running back around the building to deliver it to Emily.

"What's his deal?" Blair asked.

"He's in love."

I finished my fries and sat, watching Blair eat and waiting for her to tell me about Brett. She was taking her time.

Of course, I wanted her to say something like "He's gay," or "He's my cousin," or even "He's my *ex*-boyfriend." But she wasn't saying anything. She was just . . . eating . . . really . . . slow. It was driving me crazy.

I stood up. "I'm going to just run over and say hi to Dennis and Emily," I said.

Blair gave me a look like, *Isn't that sort of rude?*

"I just want to see how their date is going," I told her.

Chapter Forty-five
BURGER TOSS

Dear Miz Fitz,

Why do boys punch each other?

— Perplexed

Miz Fitz sez:

Boys punch because they do not have saber teeth, venomous fangs, sharp claws, stingers, clubbed tails, tusks, hooves, or poisonous sprays with which to injure one another.

LITA

"I totally believe it," I said. "Blair's had her skanky eyes on Adam since the first day of school."

"She doesn't seem like Adam's type," Emily said.

"He's a boy. She's got a bod."

"Do you think it's like a date? Or did they just kind of run into each other?"

"I think she snagged him like a carp." I had no idea what it meant to snag a carp, but I'd heard the expression someplace.

"Maybe she's helping him with his calculus," Emily said.

Dennis, meanwhile, sat there silently watching Emily and me talk, head swinging back and forth.

"Dennis, close your mouth!" I said.

His teeth came together with an audible *clack*.

"What were they doing?" Emily asked.

"Just sitting," Dennis said with a shrug. Then he looked past me and his eyes widened.

"Hey, Adam," he said.

I turned. The first thing I saw was the nasty bruise on the bridge of Adam's nose. His left eye was beginning to blacken. I looked past him. No Blair.

"What's going on?" Adam said.

"Emily and Lita are trying to figure out how come you're with Blair," Dennis said.

Adam said, "We just —"

I interrupted him. "It's no mystery at all. Plagiarists prefer the skanky type."

Adam looked at me. "What's your problem?"

"You are."

"I don't get you at all," he said.

"Right. 'Cause you're only an expert on what *boys* want."

He said, "I thought we were friends, and all of a sudden you turn into this book-throwing Blair-hating Bogzillian bitch creature."

ADAM

Okay, so it was the wrong thing to say. I guess I thought throwing "Bogzillian" in there would make it funny. Because it was originally her word. My mistake.

"Maybe because *you* turned into a complete *asshole*," Lita said, her voice getting louder. "Maybe 'cause you decided to steal somebody else's writing and pass it off as your own and act like some big-shot author. I can't believe Joe Wilkins ever let your book in his store."

"Thanks to you, he won't — until I prove to him that I really wrote it. Which I *did*, by the way."

"Bull*shit*! You ripped off half of it from Miz Fitz, and probably the rest of it from someplace else. You're pathetic. No wonder you're hanging out with *her*."

She pointed. I turned and saw Blair approaching.

"You're acting crazy, Leeter —"

"Don't tell me how I'm acting, and don't call me 'Leeter'!" She stepped toward me, jabbing her forefinger at my chest. I backed away. "Don't tell me anything! You don't *know* anything. You know nothing about girls, you know nothing about *boys*. The only thing you know about is Adam Merchant."

I backed away some more, but she kept coming at me. "Lita, just calm down, would you please?"

"Shut *up*! *God*, I can't believe I ever listened to anything you said. Did you ever have an original thought in your life? Or did you steal it all?"

"Look, Lita, okay, maybe I copied a few parts of the book, but I *rewrote* them. Besides, you're taking this all way too personal."

"*Personal?*" Lita's face was pink, and her eyes were bright with tears. She had backed me most of the way across the parking lot. People had to be gawking at us, but I was afraid to take my eyes off Lita. "*Personal?* You're not only pathetic, you're ignorant." My back hit something — a wooden fence. I had run out of backing-up room, and Lita was madder than ever. She thumped my chest with her forefinger. "You." *Thump.* "Are." *Thump.* "Stupid." *Thump.*

I never liked being called stupid, and nobody likes being thumped in the chest, so I reached out and sort of pushed her away. I must have shoved pretty hard, because she fell down. In an instant, she was back on her feet and coming at me. I dodged to the left and grabbed her wrist. She swung at me with her other hand. I caught that wrist, too, then pushed her back against the fence.

"Calm down, damn it!" I said. Or maybe I shouted it.

Lita was red-faced and furious. She tried to kick me but I got my hip up against hers, pinning her to the fence.

"You *stole,*" she said. Her eyes were wet.

"I did not! And even if I did, I didn't steal from *you*," I said. She twisted and jerked — it was like trying to hang on to an insane bobcat.

"Yes, you *did*!" She tried again to pull her hands free, but I held on — and suddenly she stopped struggling. "When you steal from Miz Fitz, you steal from me," she said.

I didn't get it at first.

And then I did. It all made sense.

"Hey," said a voice I didn't recognize. I felt a hand clamp on to my arm. In an instant, I was yanked away from Lita and *thrown*. As I hit the parking lot with my shoulder, I saw who had done the throwing.

The GTO guy. *Brett.*

What happened next — I've tried since to sort it out, but it still gets all muddled — was like a gigantic thunderstorm in my head. First there was the mental H-bomb of realizing that Lita was Miz Fitz, and the instant sick feeling that came with it, and the sense of betrayal that she hadn't told me she was Miz Fitz before, and anger over being left out, all of that floating on top of the lake of adrenaline in my gut from fighting with Lita, and beneath that the few shreds of power left over from all the attention I'd got at the book party, and from talking with Blair, and thinking maybe she really liked me, and then getting grabbed and thrown by Brett — who also had something going with Blair — and then hitting that hard asphalt . . . I bounced up off the parking lot with that whirlwind of crap in my head.

I wanted to hit somebody.

Part of me was aware of the gathering crowd. I didn't care about them. I was completely focused on Brett. I hadn't been in a fistfight since I was eight years old, but I didn't hesitate. I ran at him and swung, wanting nothing more than to ram my fist through his face to the back of his skull.

My fist didn't connect. Instead, a sledgehammer pounded my midsection, lifting me off my feet, and an instant later I was flat on my back on the cold asphalt, gasping for breath. Faces swam into view: Lita looking down at me with a shocked expression, then Dennis, openmouthed, and Stuey Herrell — where had *he* come from? Excited voices swirled in my ears, I turned my head to see Blair shoving Brett in the chest and screaming at him. Great — my date was defending me.

"Adam?" Dennis's voice. "Are you okay?"

"I'm fine," I managed to croak. I rolled over onto my hands and knees. I could see feet, at least a dozen pairs of shoes surrounding me. It was better than looking at their faces. A spasm rolled up my abdomen and flattened my stomach, sending a ragged mass of undigested burger and fries up my throat and out my mouth.

"Ga-ross," I heard. I'm pretty sure it was Tracy Spink.

Chapter Forty-six
RELATIVITY

Miz Fitz,

If my boyfriend would just once say "I'm sorry, I was wrong," I think I would die and go to heaven.

— Hellbound, a Lass

Miz Fitz sez:

You should wish for something realistic, like world peace.

LITA

A few months earlier I wrote this thing in my blog about why boys hit each other. I don't remember exactly what I wrote, but I remember thinking it was funny.

Believe me, there is nothing funny about guys hitting each other.

I've witnessed three boy-fights in my life. It's like watching humans devolve into apes. I could almost see their brows collapse and their arms elongate to knuckle-dragging length. Five million years of evolution gone in a flash.

The fight between Brett and Adam lasted only about one second. Brett hit Adam so hard I was afraid he'd never get up, but he did. As soon as I saw that Adam was breathing again, I looked around for Brett.

He was with Blair. She was shouting and shoving him while he tried to fend her off.

I wanted to yell at him, too. I ran toward them, but stopped when I heard what Blair was saying.

"— jerk! Why do you have to beat up the one guy in the whole stupid school I like?"

"But *he* came at *me*!" Brett said.

"You didn't have to hit him so hard!"

"It wasn't that hard —"

"You're supposed to *protect* me, not beat up my boyfriends!"

"I'm sorry. Look, I'm sure he's okay. I —" Brett noticed me standing behind Blair. "Lita."

Blair whirled. "You're just as bad," she said to me.

"Is that so?" I said. If she made one move toward me I . . . I wasn't sure what I'd do.

Brett said, "Take it easy, Blairbear."

I looked from Blair to Brett. A pet name. He even had a *pet name* for her.

"*Blairbear?*" I said.

Brett shrugged. "I've called her that since we were little. I couldn't pronounce Blair."

I don't know what I looked like at that moment, but Blair started laughing. She said to Brett, "She doesn't get it. She thinks I'm, like, lusting after your scrawny ass."

ADAM

After I barfed, a whole bunch of things happened that I couldn't keep track of. There was a lot of talking and shouting, and a man wearing an apron was telling everybody to get back in their cars, and Dennis was leaning over me asking if I was okay, and I heard people laughing.

I just stared down at my own vomit and wished for them all to go away, but Dennis kept pulling on my arm, trying to get me to stand up. Since there was no avoiding it, I wiped my mouth on my sleeve and sat back on my heels and found about a dozen pairs of eyes and one camcorder staring at me. Sam Johnson was behind the camcorder.

"You sure you're okay?" Dennis asked.

"I'm fine," I tried to look around without meeting anybody's eyes. I saw Bree Feider standing with Yola Garfield, talking to a couple of their no-neck letter-jacketed admirers. Robbie and Bob were watching from the jump seats in the back of Stuey Herrell's pickup truck. Stuey, leaning against the tailgate, had his arm draped around Tracy Spink's shoulders. Tracy *Spink*? Brianna Blackmun was taking food orders — apparently, parking-lot fights were business as usual.

I looked for Blair. She was halfway across the parking lot, talking with Lita and Brett.

Dennis tugged on my arm again. I shook him off and managed to stand by myself, the pain in my belly offset by the agony of my humiliation.

"You want a ride home?" Dennis asked.

"I don't want to mess up your date."

"I think I messed it up all by myself," he said, looking over at Emily, who was watching us from Dennis's mom's minivan. "She's being kind of weird."

"So go talk to her," I said.

"I don't know what to say. Every time I try to do something for her, she gets all pissy."

I was in no mood to listen to Dennis's romantic woes. I gave him a shove in Emily's direction.

"I don't —"

"Don't think," I said. Following my own advice, I headed toward Lita, Blair, and Brett, trying to walk as upright as possible. As I approached, I realized the three of them were arguing.

"Adam, too?" I heard Brett say to Blair. Blair nodded, then both she and Brett started laughing. Lita's cheeks were turning pink. I stopped a few feet away and waited for them to notice me.

Brett saw me first — he tensed up, ready to go a second round.

"Hey . . ." he said.

I nodded in a nonthreatening way. I did not need another shot in the gut. Brett relaxed slightly.

Blair was looking at me intently. "Are you okay?" she asked.

"Embarrassed," I said. I stepped up to Lita and said, "I'm sorry." I could tell from the way her eyes were all slitty and her chin stuck out that one sorry was not going to do it. In fact, she looked like she was going to explode all over again.

Blair must have seen it, too, because she stepped in between us and turned me toward Brett and said, "Adam, this is Brett Andrews." She looked at Lita. "My brother."

Chapter Forty-seven
APOLOGIES

Q: This guy I've been seeing won't admit when he's wrong. For example, he told me that Tiger Woods used to be married to Britney Spears, which is totally not true. So I showed him on Britney's website he was wrong but he just kept saying, "That doesn't prove anything." What's up with that?

A: So, when did Britney and Tiger get divorced? Just kidding. My advice is to move on — discuss the engagement between Clint Eastwood and Miley Cyrus instead. Seriously — let him slide and go do something fun.

— **from** *What Boys Want*

ADAM

For about three seconds, nobody said anything. Then Brett broke the silence. "Sorry I hit you, dude. It was reflex."

"No problem," I said, feeling numb. I looked at Lita. "You're going out with Blair's brother?"

I realized from her expression that she hadn't known about the brother-sister thing, either. There was this incredibly awkward moment — and then I laughed. Brett started laughing, too.

Wrong thing to do.

Lita spun on her heel and walked off as fast as a person can walk without running.

Brett looked at me and Blair. "What just happened?" he asked.

Blair shook her head pityingly. "Clueless men," she said.

Brett took off after Lita.

I said, still processing, "He's your *brother*?"

"Half brother."

"I thought —"

"Never mind," said Blair. She hooked her arm around my elbow. "Let's go."

"Go where?"

"Does it matter?"

I looked around and caught several people watching us.

"No," I said. "It really doesn't."

LITA

Brett caught up with me half a block down the street. I didn't slow down. He didn't say a word, just fell in beside me on my left and matched my speed, which was considerable. It was the right move, because at that point almost anything might have turned me back into the hitting, kicking, clawing Bogzillian bitch creature. Either that or I'd start crying.

We walked for what seemed like a long time but it was probably only a minute or two.

"I wasn't laughing at you," he said.

"That's okay." I could feel myself calming down. "It *was* kind of funny."

"Are you cold?"

And suddenly I *was* cold. I was *freezing*. And my feet were killing me.

He took off his sport coat and draped it over my thin denim jacket. "There," he said. "*Très* chic."

I laughed. Or maybe it was a sob. He put his arm around my shoulders.

"Adam is a good friend of yours, isn't he?"

"I've known him since, like, forever."

"He seems like a nice guy."

"He *is* a nice guy — except when he's a self-involved jerk."

"I can be a self-involved jerk, too, sometimes."

I looked at Brett. "You wouldn't steal from me."

"True. But from what I heard back there, he didn't know it was your blog he was copying from. I don't even think he understood that what he did was wrong."

I shrugged off his arm.

"Why are you defending him?"

"I just . . . look, if I ever screw up — and I guarantee I will — I'd like to think you'd give me a chance. That's all."

My mouth started to argue with him, but nothing came out. I had used up all of whatever it was that had made me want to fight. I was nothing but an empty girl standing on an empty street with a guy she hardly knew, tired from her brain to her blistered feet, wanting nothing more than to close her eyes and click her heels three times and be home in bed.

"Are you okay?" he asked, cupping my shoulders in his hands.

"No," I said, staring at his chest. He put one hand under my chin and slowly tipped my head back so I was looking straight into his eyes.

Then he kissed me. It was the softest, gentlest of kisses, and for one very confusing moment I thought that it had happened in my imagination.

"I'm sorry tonight was so awful for you," he said. Then he kissed me again a little harder. I could feel that one all the way down to my toes.

"It's getting better," I said.

ADAM

I walked Blair home, close and slow, bumping shoulders but not holding hands. She told me about Brett, and how they'd grown up together.

"Brett's real father died in a work accident when Brett was just a month old. My mom got married again a year later and had me right away. I was thirteen when I found out Brett and I had different dads. That was when he changed his name from Thompson back to Andrews, his biological dad's name."

"What happened to *your* dad?"

"My mom divorced him three years ago. He was a jerk. Lives in Texas now, I think. After the divorce we couldn't afford to live in our old house, and then I got into trouble at school — the paper-writing thing I told you about — so we moved here. My mother's taste in men sucks, in case you haven't figured that out already." She stopped walking. "Oh, crap. Speaking of jerks . . ."

We were standing in front of a small rambler on Holden Avenue. All the lights were out. The cab end of a semi was parked in the driveway.

"Ronnie's here," Blair said, looking at the truck.

"Is that the guy you were telling me about?"

"My mom's latest jerkball boyfriend, yeah."

"You want to stay at my house tonight?"

Blair shook her head. "All the lights are out, so they're probably asleep. I'll be okay."

"You sure? We've got a pullout sofa in the den."

She didn't move or say anything for what seemed like a long time. Then her shoulders sank and I realized she'd been holding herself all stiff and tense.

She said, "Okay. The Hotel Merchant it is."

When we got to my house my parents were asleep — or pretending to be asleep — so I got some fresh sheets from the linen closet and brought them downstairs to the den.

I found Blair a toothbrush, then put the sheets on the sofa bed while she made noise in the bathroom. A few minutes later she came into the den, her face free of makeup.

"Lot of books," she said, looking at the floor-to-ceiling bookshelves.

"My dad's a big reader," I said. "He likes to read about dead presidents and wars and stuff."

"I think they call that *history*," said Blair.

"Exactly."

She plopped down on the edge of the bed and started unlacing her boots.

"I still can't believe that Lita is Miz Fitz," she said. "I read her blog a few times. She's funny." Blair looked up at me. "You think she'll ever forgive you?"

I puffed out my cheeks, shaking my head slowly. "I don't know. When we were little kids I once shot her with a slingshot." I sat down next to Blair. "She still brings it up."

"So you two have a violent history," said Blair.

"I guess. But we always stayed friends. At least till now." My arm came up and settled on Blair's shoulder.

She let her head fall back, looking up at the ceiling. "You don't want to get involved with me." She turned her head, and we looked at each other from inches away.

"Why not?"

"Because I may have inherited my mother's bad taste in men."

"In other words, if you like me, I must be a jerk?"

"Something like that."

"Do you know you look fantastic without your makeup?"

She gave me a suspicious look, trying to figure out if I was mocking her.

"You really do," I said, and then I kissed her.

. . .

The next morning my mother found us wrapped around each other on the sofa bed. Fortunately — or not, depending on your point of view — we still had our clothes on. I woke up with my mother wiggling my foot. She waited until I sat up.

"Do we have a shortage of beds in this house?" she asked.

"Um . . . we were . . ." I looked at Blair. Her eyes were wide open. "We were talking, and I guess we fell asleep," I said.

"Talking? Is that what they call it now?" My mom shook her head and went out to the kitchen and started banging pots and pans around. Blair and I looked at each other. At first I thought she was going to get hysterical, but instead she started to giggle, and within seconds we were both convulsed with silent laughter.

Chapter Forty-eight
STROKES AND LASHES

I regret to report that due to events beyond Miz Fitz's control, this blog has temporarily (or perhaps permanently) suspended publication.

— The Exhausted and Misunderstood Miz Fitz

LITA

Monday morning I realized that I had made a huge, gargantuan, life-destroying mistake.

The advantage of an anonymous blog is you can write anything you want with no repercussions outside the blog itself. The anonymous Miz Fitz was happy to offer her unexpurgated opinions on matters ranging from religion to politics to sex to personal hygiene, and no one accused her of being stupid or cruel or thoughtless or ignorant or slanderous. At least not in person.

But that all changed once my secret identity became public knowledge.

I'd had all weekend to censor my own blog and I hadn't done it. Why?

I wanted to leave it up so people could see for themselves how much Adam had stolen from me. Bad, bad, *bad* idea.

It's one thing to blog anonymously that girls who use Impulse body spray are "desperate, tasteless hos," or that the guys on the football team are all trying desperately to compensate for their lack of sexual prowess. It was another thing altogether to run into those same people in the hall and have them know it was me who said those things.

By the afternoon, I was seriously considering changing schools. I was at my locker grabbing a few books and planning to skip out for the rest of the day when Adam came creeping up and started apologizing. As he stood there telling me what a pathetic ass he was, I realized I was hardly mad at him at all anymore. I actually felt sorry for him. The poor guy had two black eyes, and his big publishing venture had turned out to be a complete and utter embarrassment, and he was stuck with a bunch of books that he couldn't sell. In a way, we were pariahs together. I kept remembering something Brett had said: *Look, if I ever screw up — and I guarantee I will — I'd like to think you'd give me a chance.* Not that I was ready to forgive and forget. But I could feel his pain.

I made it out of the school without incident and went straight home. My mom was back in her study typing away on a new book. The cycle was about to repeat itself. I ran upstairs, switched on my computer, and proceeded to shut down my blog.

Ten minutes later my phone rang. It was Brett.

"Hey," he said, "how come you took your blog off-line?"

"You can't have read very much of it if you're asking me that."

"I read most of it. I thought it was great."

I closed my eyes, thinking of all the potentially embarrassing things he might have read.

"I especially liked the part about the art of seduction —"

That was one.

"— and feminine hygiene secrets."

"Shut *up!*" I said.

Brett laughed. "Seriously, it's brilliant. You should turn it into a book and publish it."

"Yeah, then everybody would say I was copying Adam. They already hate me. I'd rather not make things worse."

ADAM

Monday morning at school was okay, at first. I got plenty of strokes for the book. A lot of people had read it and liked it, and nobody seemed to have a big problem with the fact that I'd copied some of it. I could have sold a few dozen more books, except for one little problem: Gerald Hanson, my dad's lawyer.

Gerald Hanson had stopped by the house on Sunday afternoon at my father's request. He sat at my computer for an hour, reading Miz Fitz's blog and comparing it to sections from my book. Every now and then he would sigh and shake his head and make a note on his PDA.

Afterward, he sat down with us in the living room and told us that the changes I'd made to Miz Fitz's writing were not "sufficient" to make my book an original work. Unless I could get permission from the author of the blog, he told me, I would be risking legal action if I continued to sell the book.

"She's your friend. You need to talk to her," said my mother.

Gerald Hanson agreed. "But don't admit to anything in front of witnesses," he added.

I caught Lita at her locker Monday afternoon and launched into my apology. I figured if I apologized enough, eventually it would have an effect. Lita listened, staring at me with a flat, blank look that could have meant anything. I said I was sorry about six different ways, searching for any sign of softening in her eyes.

"What exactly do you want, Adam?" she asked after I ran out of sorrys.

"I'm not selling any more books," I said.

"You mean you *can't* sell any more books. I heard about your lawyer."

"Oh." I had made the mistake of telling Bob Glaus about Gerald Hanson, and he had told Robbie, who told his sister, who told . . . you get the picture.

I said, "How about if I pay you a percentage?"

"For you to sell *my* words in a book with *your* name on it?"

"How about —"

"Adam, just leave it alone." She peered closely at my face, which was looking raccoon-like from the book bruise. "Sorry about the nose."

"It's okay. I probably deserved it."

Lita nodded, very serious. "Yeah, you did."

I figured I'd wait a couple more days, then try her again.

As for Blair, I hadn't heard from her since she'd left my house Sunday morning. I'd tried calling her and texting her, but she wasn't getting back to me. I figured her phone was broken or something, but she hadn't shown up at school, either. I wasn't exactly frantic with worry, but I kept going back over that night we spent at my house, trying to remember if I'd done or said something wrong. Lately, my record hadn't been too good.

Things were not going so well for Dennis and Emily, either. They had officially broken up after just one date. I stopped by Dennis's house after school to get the details. To my surprise, he was not at all upset. He had bought his new game system and was deep into *Resistance*. It was all he could do to acknowledge my presence.

"Girls take a lot of time, effort, and money," he said as he blew away a Howler with a grenade. "Anyway, I think she's more interested in Sam Johnson now."

Sam Johnson hardly knew that Emily existed. I guess from Emily's point of view, that made him all that much more appealing. Sam was more interested in *me*, as in dragging my name through the mud. Go online and search for "Teen Horking Video." Yeah, that's me. I could hardly wait to see the next issue of the *Wellstone Word*.

I tried calling Blair about ten times that night. No answer. After the third call, I quit leaving messages.

By Tuesday, every single student at Wellstone had heard various versions of how I'd copied my entire book from Lita's blog, and how that made me the most evil creature in the universe. It got to where people wouldn't even meet my eye, like they were embarrassed to associate with me. It was completely unfair, because even though about half of my book came from Miz Fitz, I was the one who put it all together. And the other half was mostly original.

Lita was having her own problems. The news that Lita was Miz Fitz was just as sensational as the news about me being a plagiarist. As Miz Fitz, Lita had posted some pretty outrageous stuff about the students and faculty at Wellstone. She'd be paying for it for a long time.

Wednesday, Blair was still not in school. That afternoon I went over to her house. The semi cab was still parked in the driveway. A man with a long, reddish-gray ponytail, faded jeans, and a black denim jacket, was scrubbing road tar off the chrome wheels.

"Nice rig," I said.

"Thanks." He went back to cleaning his wheels. A few seconds later he looked up again. "Something I can do you for?"

"Is Blair around?" I asked.

"Haven't seen her."

An older, white Nissan pulled up to the curb. A nice-looking middle-aged woman wearing a Fleet Farm shirt climbed out and took a bag of groceries from the backseat.

"You still here?" she said to the man.

He ignored her and went back to polishing his chrome.

"If you're not gone in half an hour I'm calling the cops," she said, and headed for the front door.

I called after her. "Mrs. Thompson?"

She stopped on the steps and turned to face me. I could see her resemblance to Blair — but thirty years older, and without the makeup and black leather.

"My name's Adam Merchant," I said. "I'm a friend of Blair's. I haven't seen her in a few days and I was just wondering . . . is she okay?"

"She's staying with her aunt in Saint Paul." Looking past me at the red-haired man, Blair's mother said, "I mean it, Ronnie! I want you out of here."

The man gave her the finger and continued to clean his wheels.

"Do you have a phone number for her?" I asked.

"You said your name was Adam?"

I nodded.

She shifted the bag of groceries to one arm and opened the door with the other. "I'll tell her you stopped by." She stepped inside and closed the door.

As I was walking away, the man called after me. "Hey, kid."

I stopped.

"They turn on ya," he said. "Women."

Chapter Forty-nine
A VERY TALENTED YOUNG MAN

Choosing the perfect gift for a guy could not be easier. A Ferrari, candy-apple red, would be a good choice. Even if you don't have a couple hundred thousand dollars to spend, any device featuring buttons, switches, and dials is sure to please.

— **from** *What Boys Want*

ADAM

I thought about what Ronnie the trucker said all the way home — the thing about women turning on you — and for the first few blocks I sort of agreed with him. Lita had turned on me, and Emily had turned on Dennis, and now Blair's mom wouldn't give me Blair's aunt's phone number — but when I thought about it some more, I realized that it wasn't just the women. It was everybody turning on everybody. If Blair's mom kicked out Ronnie the trucker, it was probably because of something he had done. And when Lita turned on me — well, I had to admit she had her reasons. But what about Blair? The last time I'd seen her was when I'd dropped her off at home Sunday morning. She'd kissed me good-bye, and everything had seemed cool. So why hadn't she called me?

I kept checking my phone, then I tried to think of who I could call. Would any of Blair's lunch-table crowd know where to find her? Then it hit me. Brett. Brett would know. But how could I find Brett?

For that, I would have to call Lita.

I was trying to get up the nerve to dial Lita's number when the phone rang. I snatched it up.

"Hello?"

"May I speak with Mr. Adam Merchant, please?"

It wasn't a voice I recognized, and she had called me "mister," so I figured she wanted to sell me vinyl siding or something.

I said, "We live in a tent." I love to give them a hard time.

"Excuse me?"

"We live in a tent. We don't need any siding. Or gutters. Or windows. Or whatever it is you're selling."

"I'm sorry — am I speaking to Adam Merchant?"

"Yes, and we don't want any."

"Adam Merchant, the author of *What Boys Want*?"

Oops. Not a siding seller, apparently.

"Uh, yeah?"

"Mr. Merchant, this is Tess Ormen from Sprole, Cass, and Tish in New York."

Sprole, Cass, and Tish? I'd heard the name someplace, but I couldn't think of where.

"What's Sprole, Cass, and Tish?" I asked.

"We are a publishing company."

"Oh." I'd seen their name on books.

"You *are* Adam Merchant?"

"Yeah. Uh, what can I do for you, Ms. Orton?"

"*Ormen.* Tess Ormen. You can call me Tess."

"Okay. You can call me Adam."

"Adam, I'm calling because I just read your book, and I think it's brilliant."

Brain freeze — I saw the word like a neon sign:

BRILLIANT!

"I'm sorry . . . you read my book? In New York?"

She laughed. "Yes, we do that here."

"I mean, how did it get to New York?"

"One of my authors sent it to me. Do you know Amanda Maize?"

"No."

"Her real name is Amanda Wold."

"Oh! Lita's mom!"

"Yes, she sent it to me, I read it, and I wanted to let you know how much I liked it."

"Thank you."

"It's a remarkable little piece. May I ask how many copies you've sold?"

"Quite a few," I said. "More than a hundred."

"Really! That's wonderful! How old are you?"

"Seventeen," I said.

"You are a very talented young man."

TALENTED!

"Adam, the reason I'm calling is because we would like to publish *What Boys Want*."

"But . . . I already published it."

"Yes, and you've sold one-hundred-plus copies, which is very respectable for a self-published book. But if we were to publish it here at SCT, we might be able to sell tens of *thousands* of them. Of course, we would offer you a generous advance. Do you have an agent?"

I think that was the point where my mind went blank. I must have said something, but I can't remember what. Probably something about needing to talk to my parents. At least I had the wits to scribble down Tess Ormen's name and phone number, then get off the phone. I stood there shaking for about a minute. Was this a dream? I felt as if my chest was inflating — and then it all whooshed out of me two seconds later when I realized that it was impossible. The instant they found out that I'd copied half of the book from Lita's blog, Sprole, Cass, and Tish would dump me faster than Emily had dumped Dennis.

It was like winning the lottery, and then finding out your ticket was a counterfeit.

LITA

"I just think he's so *virile*," Emily said.

I groaned and flopped back on the couch, keeping the phone glued to my ear. "Is that going to be your new word?" I asked. *"Virile?"*

"No! But don't you think so?"

"Are we really talking about Sam Johnson?"

"Yes!"

"You're making my head hurt," I said. "What about all that work we did so you could get your hooks into Dennis?"

"Dennis didn't work out," Emily said.

"You're fickle."

"I know. I feel bad about Dennis. At least he made some money tutoring me."

"Sam Johnson is a terrible writer," I said.

"I don't care. Virility trumps literary talent."

"He was responsible for getting me kicked off the *Word*."

"Love is not rational."

"No kidding."

"How's it going with Brett?"

"I'm going to a sixties hot-rod show with him next weekend."

"And you're criticizing me for lusting after Sam because he's a lousy writer?"

She had a point. I half listened to her go on about Sam Johnson for a few more minutes, all while thinking about how little control we have over who we fall for. I'd gotten lucky with Brett. I'd started out with a mini-crush on what I thought was a dropout grease monkey, and it turned out he was a *literate* grease monkey. Even Adam had no control over his own lust-o-meter. Why else would he fall for Blair Thompson?

It occurred to me for the first time that Adam might genuinely *like* Blair. At the same time it hit me that Blair could have things in common with her brother. In other words, she might not be so bad after all.

Emily was describing how Sam Johnson had once held a door open for her. She managed to infuse the event with cosmic significance. A beep in my ear announced another caller trying to get through. I said, "I've got to take this call," and hit the TALK button.

"It's me. Don't hang up!" Adam said. "I have two questions."

I didn't say anything, but I didn't hang up.

"First, do you know how I can get hold of Brett? I'm trying to find Blair. She hasn't been in school and I'm worried."

I took a breath, then said what I'd been thinking. "I'm still mad at you about the book," I said, "but I'm sorry I was such a bitch about Blair."

"You are? You were?"

Oblivious. "Yeah, I am, and I was." I gave him Brett's cell number. "What's the second question?"

He cleared his throat and said, "How would you like to become a bestselling author?"

Chapter Fifty

BOGZILLIANS

The Countess Ravishia, who let no detail escape her, preferred her lovers to address her as *Your Grace* in the morning, *My Lady* in the afternoon, and *Your Highness* at night in the privacy of her red satin-lined boudoir.

— **from** *Wrathlust Hollow*, **by Carmelita Woldstonecraft**

ADAM

I found Blair sitting at a rickety table in the back of a coffee shop working on her laptop. I sat down across from her. She looked up and jerked in her chair like she'd been goosed. I saw the flicker of a smile come and go as fast as hands clapping. Her face instantly reverted to blasé, and she regarded me through heavily lidded, heavily made-up eyes.

"What took you so long?" she said.

"You were expecting me?"

"Not really. But it sounded like a cool thing to say." She smiled, and this time it lasted almost an entire second.

"I left you a bunch of messages," I said.

"Sorry. I left my cell at my mom's. How did you find me?"

"Your brother gave me your aunt's phone number, and your aunt told me you were hiding out here."

"Yeah, I had to get out of that house. My cousins were driving me crazy. They're six and eight, and their entire universe is playing with their Bratz dolls. They think *I'm* just a big a Bratz doll."

"How come you never called me?"

"I've been thinking."

"Your mom kicked Ronnie out."

"She does that from time to time. He'll soon be replaced by some other jerkball."

"What happened?"

"*Nothing* happened." She looked up at me, her eyes flashing. "I just didn't feel like going home and dealing with Ronnie and my mom."

"What about me?"

"What *about* you?"

"I thought we . . . you know."

"What, you thought I was going to be your *girlfriend*? Because we made out?" She laughed, but not like she thought it was funny. "I suppose you've already told everybody at school that you slept with me."

"No! I wouldn't do that! Anyway, it's not true. I mean, we slept together *literally*, but not *actually*."

"Since when did what's true or actual make any difference to anybody?" Blair closed her laptop and leaned back in her chair. Neither of us spoke for a few seconds.

"Are you coming back to Wellstone?"

Blair shrugged. "Probably. I can only take so many conversations about Sasha and Yasmin Bratz's fashion feud." She picked up her empty coffee cup and looked into it, frowning. "Do you ever worry you're going to turn out just like your parents?"

"I never thought about it," I said.

"Every time I ever get involved with a guy, he turns into a jerk. It's a family trait. Look at my mom. Or my brother, all in lust after your Bogzillian bitch creature, or whatever it was you called her."

"Lita's not so bad," I said. "She had good reason to be mad at me. Anyway, we're working on a project together. We . . . um . . . we're going to do the book together." I started to tell her about the call from Tess Ormen, but before I got very far, I noticed that Blair was examining her paper coffee cup as if it was the most fascinating thing in the world. "What?" I said.

Blair gave the faintest possible shrug. "So you'll be spending a lot of time with her?"

"Not as much as I hope to spend with you," I said. It was a good line, I thought.

Blair turned the cup in her hand, frowning, then set it aside. After about thirty seconds she said, "Like I told you before, you don't want to get involved with me."

"Oh yes, I do."

We stared at each other — it seemed like forever — then I said, "I was thinking we could go out tonight. You and me."

"A *date*?" She tried for her blasé look, but it didn't take. "What did you have in mind?"

"Does it matter?"

"Maybe. If you tell me you're taking me bungee jumping, I'll know not to wear a skirt."

"No bungee jumping. I was thinking dinner and a movie."

Blair nodded slowly. "Okay," she said. "I can do that."

LITA

"I'm going to have to rewrite a lot of this," I said as I paged through Adam's book.

"Of course you will," said my mother. "Your name will be on the cover."

"Do you think we'll have to go on a book tour or anything?" I asked.

"I imagine so. Book signings, readings, the whole package. Tess likes to give her first-time authors a big push." My mother sipped her coffee — she always took a break from her writing mid-afternoon for a cappuccino — and gave me a Proud Mother smile. "Tess thinks your book could be a big hit. It will probably outsell the latest Amanda Maize romance."

"She wants us to put up a website. Kind of like Miz Fitz, only with both me and Adam answering questions."

"That sounds like a fun project."

"Do you think Tess might publish my novel, too?"

The semi-famous Amanda Maize sat back in her chair, as startled as I'd ever seen her. "You've written a novel?"

"Half written."

She shook her head in amazement. "I had no idea I'd raised a Mary Shelley."

"Who?"

"Mary Shelley wrote *Frankenstein* when she wasn't much older than you. What is your novel called?"

I blushed, but told her, anyway. "*Wrathlust Hollow.*"

My mother threw her head back and roared.

"It's just a working title," I said.

"No! It's great. The perfect companion piece to *What Boys Want.*"

I frowned at the book cover with the big question mark. "I'm thinking about changing Adam's title."

"Why? It's perfect."

"Just a minor adjustment," I said. "I'm sure Adam won't mind."

My mother cocked an eyebrow. "Don't forget, he's got as much invested in this as you do."

"I know." I sighed. "I suppose I'll have to spend a lot of time working with him."

"Is that so bad?"

"No . . . except I wonder how Brett will like it."

"If Brett is worth keeping, he'll be fine with you and Adam working together."

"He's a guy. He has built-in testosterone issues."

My mother chuckled. "Maybe you'll have to add a chapter about that in the book."

Epilogue
WHAT BOYS REALLY WANT

Hi, Adam! Hi, Lita!

My BF is fabulously wealthy and he buys me expensive stuff all the time. How do I find out if he really likes me?

Pampered but Perplexed

Dear Pampered,

Ask him to tattoo your name on his forehead.

— **from the** *What Boys Really Want* **website**

ADAM

I'm not going to say how big our check from the publisher was, but Lita and I took Brett and Blair out in a limo to celebrate. We had dinner at La Belle Vie — food so fancy and French you wouldn't know it was food if you weren't paying, like, five bucks a bite. Both Lita and Blair looked amazing, Brett was so mature and debonair I felt like I should be taking notes. I was just happy to get through the meal without spilling anything down my shirt. After dinner, we went to First Avenue to see a band called Binky Stud — Brett knew the bass player. I embarrassed myself on the dance floor and had a great time. Later, over coffee drinks at the Bitter Bean, Lita and Blair got into a discussion about what boys really want.

"They want to be worshipped," Lita said. "They want a girl to look at them and see perfection."

"In other words, they want a mindless fool," said Blair.

Brett and I looked at each other.

"Not exactly," Lita said. "They look into a girl's eyes and they want to see their ideal self reflected. In other words, they want somebody who will make them feel good about themselves."

"I like that," Blair said. "You should put it in your book."

"Oh, it's in there," Lita said with a broad grin. "This time, we didn't leave anything out."

Blair made her eyes go big. "I hope you left *some* things out!"

"Just the boring parts." Lita turned to me and winked.

I winked back.

Brett and Blair, with one voice, said, "Hey!"

ACKNOWLEDGMENTS

What Boys Really Want was conceived as a he-said/she-said story written with fellow author Mary Logue, with each of us writing alternate scenes. The idea was that I would handle Adam's parts, while Mary would write in Lita's voice.

"It will be fun!" I said, channeling Adam Merchant. Mary wasn't so sure about the "fun" part, but she agreed to give it a try. I sketched out an outline, and we began to write.

Four chapters later it wasn't fun anymore. I think the problem was that I had come up with the concept for the book, and Mary, whose mind is as creative, active, and dangerous as Lita's, decided she would rather be working on her own ideas. Also, I tend to be somewhat directive. Okay, pushy.

Mary and I agreed that it was no fun at all to do things that weren't fun, so we abandoned the project and went to work on our own books.

A few years later I reread those early chapters of *What Boys Really Want*, and asked Mary's permission to have a go at it alone. "Knock yourself out," she said, or words to that effect.

I made a bunch of changes in what we'd written, and I took the story in a slightly new direction, but many of Mary's words and phrases have survived my edits. Specifically, many of Lita's best lines in the first four chapters were written by Mary Logue.

Thank you, Mary. I love you. Please don't sue me.